NELL GWYNNE'S

SCARLET SPY

NELL GWYNNE'S
SCARLET SPY

Kage Baker

Illustrated by J. K. Potter

FAR TERRITORIES 2010

First Edition

ISBN
978-1-59606-325-9

Far Territories
PO Box 190106
Burton, MI 48519

ONE:

In which it is established that:

IN THE CITY of Westminster, in the vicinity of Birdcage Walk, in the year of our Lord 1844...

There was once a private residence with a view of St. James' park. It was generally known, among the London tradesmen, that a respectable widow resided there, upon whom it was never necessary to call for overdue payment. Beggars knew she could be relied upon for charity, if they weren't too importunate, and they were careful never to be so; for she was one of their own, in a manner of speaking, being as she was blind.

Now and again Mrs. Corvey could be observed, with her smoked goggles and walking-stick, on the arm of her adolescent son Herbert, taking the pleasant air in the park. It was known that she had several daughters also, though the precise number was unclear, and that her younger sister was in residence there as well. There may even have been a pair of younger sisters, or perhaps there was an unmarried sister-in-law, and though the daughters had certainly left the schoolroom their governess seemed to have been retained.

In any other neighborhood, perhaps, there would have been some uncouth speculation about the inordinate number of females under one roof. The lady of the house by Birdcage Walk, however, retained her reputation for spotless respectability, largely because no gentlemen visitors were ever seen arriving or departing the premises, at any hour of the day or night whatsoever.

Gentlemen were unseen because they never went to the house near Birdcage Walk. They went instead to a certain private establishment known as Nell Gwynne's, two streets away, which connected to Mrs. Corvey's cellar by an underground passage and which was in the basement of a fairly exclusive dining establishment. The tradesmen never came near *that* place, needless to say. Had any one of them ever done so, he'd have been astonished to meet there Mrs. Corvey and her entire household, including Herbert, who under this separate roof was transformed, Harlequin-like, into Herbertina. The other ladies resident were likewise transformed from Ladies into Women, brandishing riding crops, birch rods and other instruments of their profession.

Nell Gwynne's clientele were often statesmen, who found the place convenient to Whitehall. They were not infrequently members of other exclusive clubs. Some were journalists. Some were notable persons in the sciences or the arts. All were desperately grateful to have been accorded membership at Nell Gwynne's, for it was known—among the sort of gentlemen who know such things—that there was no use whining for a sponsor. Membership was by invitation only, and entirely at the discretion of the lady whose establishment it was.

Now and again, in the hushed and circumspect atmosphere of the Athenaeum (or the Carlton Club, or the Traveller's Club) someone might imbibe enough port to wonder aloud just what it took to get an invitation from Mrs. Corvey.

The answer, though quite simple, was never guessed.

One had to know secrets.

*S*ECRETS WERE, IN fact, the principal item retailed at Nell Gwynne's, with entertainments of the flesh coming in a distant second. Secrets were teased out of sodden members of Parliament, coaxed from lustful cabinet ministers, extracted from talkative industrialists, and finessed from members of the Royal Society as well as the British Association for the Advancement of Science.

Information so acquired was not, as you might expect, sold to the highest bidder. It went directly across Whitehall and up past Scotland Yard, to an unimposing-looking brick edifice in Craig's Court, wherein was housed Redking's Club. Membership at Redking's was composed equally of other MPs, ministers, industrialists and Royal Society members, and a great many other clever fellows beside. However, there were many more clever fellows beneath Redking's, for *its* secret cellars went down several storeys, and housed an organization known publicly—but to very few—as the Gentlemen's Speculative Society.

In return for the secrets sent their way by Mrs. Corvey, the GSS underwrote her establishment, enabling all ladies present to live pleasantly when they were not engaged in the business of gathering intelligence. Indeed, once a year Nell Gwynne's closed its premises when its residents went on holiday. The more poetical of the ladies preferred the Lake District, but Mrs. Corvey liked nothing better than a month at the seaside, so they generally ended up going to Torbay.

Life for the ladies of Nell Gwynne's was, placed in the proper historical, societal and economic context, quite tolerably nice.

Now and then it did have its challenges, however.

TWO:

In which our Heroine is a Witness to History

W E WILL CALL her Lady Beatrice, since that was the name she chose for herself later.

*L*ADY BEATRICE'S PAPA was a military man, shrewd and sober. Lady Beatrice's Mamma was a gently-bred primrose of a woman, demure, proper, perfectly genteel. She was somewhat pained to discover that the daughter she bore was rather more bold and direct than became a little girl.

Lady Beatrice, encountering a horrid great spider in the garden, would not scream and run. She would stamp on it. Lady Beatrice, on having her doll snatched away by a bullying cousin, would not weep and plead; she would take back her doll, even at the cost of pulled hair and torn lace. Lady Beatrice, upon falling down, would never lie there sobbing, waiting for an adult to comfort her. She would pick herself up and inspect her knees for damage. Only when the damage amounted to bloody painful scrapes would she perhaps cry, as she limped off to the ayah to be scolded and bandaged.

Lady Beatrice's Mamma fretted, saying such brashness ill became a little lady. Lady Beatrice's Papa said he was damned glad to have a child who never wept unless she was really hurt.

"My girl's true as steel, ain't she?" he said fondly. Whereupon Lady Beatrice's Mamma would purse her lips and narrow her eyes.

Presently Lady Beatrice's Mamma had another focus for her attention, however, for walking out in the cabbage patch one day she found a pair of twin baby girls, as like her and each other as it was possible to be. Lady Beatrice hadn't thought there was a cabbage patch in the garden. She went out and searched diligently, and found not so much as a Brussels sprout, which fact she announced loudly at dinner that evening. Lady Beatrice's Mamma turned scarlet. Lady Beatrice's Papa roared with laughter.

Thereafter Lady Beatrice was allowed a most agreeable childhood, by her standards, Mamma being preoccupied with little Charlotte and Louise. She was given a pony, and was taught to ride by their Punjabi groom. She was given a bow and arrows and taught archery. She was taught her letters, and read as many books as she liked. When she asked for her own regimental uniform, Mamma told her such a thing was wicked, and retired with a fainting fit, but Papa gave her a little red coat on her next birthday.

The birthdays came and went. Just after Lady Beatrice turned seventeen, Lady Beatrice's Grandmamma was taken ill, and so Lady Beatrice's Mamma took the twins and went back to England for a visit. Lady Beatrice was uninterested in going, having several handsome young officers swooning for her at the time, and Mamma was quite content to leave her in India with Papa.

Grandmamma had been expected to die rather soon, but for some reason lingered, and Lady Beatrice's Mamma found one reason after another to postpone returning. Lady Beatrice relished running Papa's house by herself, especially presiding over dinners, where she bantered with all the handsome young officers and not a few of the old ones. One of them wrote poetry in praise of her gray eyes. Two others dueled on her account.

Then Papa's regiment was ordered to Kabul.

Lady Beatrice was left alone with the servants for some months, bored beyond anything she had believed possible. One day word came that all the wives and children of the married officers were to be allowed to go to Kabul as well, as a way to keep up the troops' morale. Lady Beatrice heard nothing directly from Papa, as it happened, but she went with all the other families. After two months of miserably difficult travel through all the red dust in the world, Lady Beatrice arrived in Kabul.

Papa was not pleased to see her. Papa was horrified. He sat her down and in few words explained how dangerous their situation was, how unlikely it was that the Afghanis would accept the British-backed ruler. He told her that rebellion was likely to break out any moment, and that the order to send for wives and children had been perfectly insane folly.

Lady Beatrice had proudly told Papa that she wasn't afraid to stay in Kabul; after all, all her handsome suitors were there! Papa had given a bitter laugh and replied that he didn't think it was safe now to send her home alone in any case.

So Lady Beatrice had stayed in Kabul, hosting Papa's dinners for increasingly glum and uninterested young suitors. She remained there until the end, when Elphinstone negotiated the retreat of the British garrison, and was one of the doomed sixteen thousand who set off from Kabul for the Khyber Pass.

Lady Beatrice watched them die, one after another after another. They died of the January cold; they died when Ghilzai snipers picked them off, or rode down in bands and skirmished with the increasingly desperate army. Papa died in the Khoord Kabul gorge, during one such skirmish, and Lady Beatrice was carried away screaming by a Ghilzai tribesman.

Lady Beatrice was beaten and raped. She was left tied among the horses. In the night she tore through the rope with her teeth and crawled into the shelter where her captors slept. She took a knife and cut their throats, and did worse to the last one, because he woke and attempted to break her wrist. She swathed herself in their garments, stole a pair of their boots. She stole their food. She took their horses, riding one and leading the others, and went down to find Papa's body.

He was frozen stiff when she found him, so she had to give up any idea of tying him across the saddle and taking him away. Instead she buried him under a cairn of stones, and scratched his name and regiment on the topmost rock with the knife with which she had killed her rapists. Then Lady Beatrice rode away, weeping; but she felt no shame weeping, because she was really hurt.

All along the Khyber Pass she counted the British and Indian dead. On three separate occasions she rode across the

body of one and then another and another of her handsome
young suitors. Lady Beatrice looked like a gray-eyed specter,
all her tears wept out, by the time she rode into Jellalabad.

No one quite knew what to do with her there. No one
wanted to speak of what had happened, for, as one of the
officers who had known her family explained, her father's
good name was at stake. Lady Beatrice remained with the
garrison all through the siege of Jellalabad that followed,
cooking for them and washing clothes. In April, just after the
siege had been raised, she miscarried.

*H*ER FATHER'S FRIENDS saw to it that Lady Beatrice was
escorted back to India. There she sold off the furniture, dismissed the servants, closed up the house and bought herself
passage to England.

*O*NCE SHE HAD arrived, it took Lady Beatrice several weeks
to find Mamma and the twins. Grandmamma had died at
last, and upon receiving word of the massacre in Afghanistan,
Mamma had bought mourning and thrown herself upon the
mercy of her older brother, a successful merchant. She and
the twins were now living as dependents in his household.

Lady Beatrice arrived on their doorstep and was greeted
by shrieks of horror. Apparently Lady Beatrice's letters had
gone astray in the mail. Her mother fainted dead away. Uncle
Frederick's wife came in and fainted dead away as well.
Charlotte and Louise came running down to see what had

happened and, while they did not faint, they screamed shrilly. Uncle Frederick came in and stared at her as though his eyes would burst from his face.

Once Mamma and Aunt Harriet had been revived, to cling to each other weeping on the settee, Lady Beatrice explained what had happened to her.

A lengthy and painful discussion followed. It lasted through tea and dinner. It was revealed to Lady Beatrice that, though she had been sincerely mourned when Mamma had been under the impression she was dead, her unexpected return to life was something more than inconvenient. Had she never considered the disgrace she would inflict upon her family by returning, after all that had happened to her? What were all Aunt Harriet's neighbors to think?

Uncle Frederick as good as told her to her face that she must have whored herself to the men of the 13th Foot, during all those months in Jellalabad; and if she hadn't, she might just as well have, for all that anyone would believe otherwise.

At this point Mamma fainted again. While they were attempting to revive her, Charlotte and Louise reproached Lady Beatrice in bluntest terms for her selfishness. Had she never thought for a moment of what the scandalous news would do to *their* marriage prospects? Mamma, sitting up at this point, tearfully begged Lady Beatrice to enter a convent. Lady Beatrice replied that she no longer believed in God.

Whereupon Uncle Frederick, his face black with rage, rose from the table (the servants were in the act of serving the fish course) and told Lady Beatrice that she would be permitted to spend the night under his roof, for her Mamma's sake, but in the morning he was personally taking her to the nearest convent.

At this point Aunt Harriet pointed out that the nearest convent was in France, and he would be obliged to drive all day and hire passage on a boat, which hardly seemed respectable. Uncle Frederick shouted that he didn't give a damn. Mamma fainted once more.

Lady Beatrice excused herself and rose from the table. She went upstairs, found her mother's room, ransacked her jewel box, and left the house by the back door.

She caught the night coach in the village and went to London, where she pawned a necklace of her mother's and paid a quarter's rent on a small room in the Marylebone Road. Having done that, Lady Beatrice went to a dressmaker's and had an ensemble made in the most lurid scarlet silk the seamstress could find on her shelves. Afterward she went to a milliner's and had a hat made up to match.

The next day she went shopping for shoes and found a pair of ready-mades in her size that looked as though they would bear well with prolonged walking. Lady Beatrice purchased cosmetics also.

When her scarlet raiment was ready Lady Beatrice collected it. She took it back to her room, put it on, and stood before the cracked glass above her washstand. Holding her head high, she rimmed her gray eyes with blackest kohl.

What else was there to do, but die?

THREE:

In which she Gets On with Her Life

THE WORK SEEMED by no means as dreadful as Lady Beatrice had heard tell. She realized, however, that her point of view was somewhat unusual. The act was never pleasurable for her but it was at least not painful, as it had been in the Khyber Pass. She took care to carry plenty of lambskin sheaths in her reticule. She worked her body like a draft horse. It obeyed her patiently and earned her decent meals and a clean place in which to sleep, and books. Lady Beatrice found that she still enjoyed books.

She felt nothing, neither for nor against, regarding the men who lay with her.

Lady Beatrice learned quickly where the best locations were for plying one's trade, if one didn't wish to be brutalized by drunken laborers: outside theaters, outside the better restaurants and wine bars. She discovered that her looks and her voice gave her an advantage over the other working women, who were for the most part desperate country girls or Cockneys. She watched them straggle through their nights, growing steadily drunker and more hoarse, sporting upper-arm bruises ever more purple.

They regarded her with disbelief and anger, especially when an old cove with a diamond stickpin could walk their importuning gauntlet unmoved, shaking off their hands, deaf to their filthiest enticements, but stop in his tracks when Lady Beatrice stepped out in front of him. "Oi! Milady's stole another one!" someone would cry. She liked the name.

One night three whores lay for her with clubs in an alley off the Strand. She pulled a knife—for she carried one—and held them at bay, and told them what she'd done to the Ghilzai tribesmen. They backed away, and fled. They spread the word that Milady was barking mad.

Lady Beatrice wasn't at all mad. It was true that the snows of the Khyber Pass seemed to have settled around her heart and left it incapable of much emotion, but her mind was sharp and clear as ice. It was difficult even to feel contempt for her fellow whores, though she saw plainly enough that many were ignorant, that they drank too much, that they habitually fell in love with men who beat them, that they wallowed in self-pity and festering resentments.

Lady Beatrice never drank. She lived thriftily. She opened a bank account and saved the money she made, reserving out enough to remain well-dressed and buy a novel now and again. She calculated how much she would need to save in order to retire and live quietly, and she worked toward that goal. She kept a resolute barrier between her body and her mind, only nominally resident in the one, only truly living in the other.

One evening she was strolling the pavement outside the British Museum (an excellent place to do business, judging from all the wealthy clientele she picked up there) when a previous customer recognized her and engaged her services for a gentlemen's party on the following night. Lady Beatrice dressed in her best evening scarlets for the occasion, and paid for a cab.

She recognized some of her better-dressed rivals at the party, at which some sporting victory was being celebrated, and they nodded to one another graciously. One by one, each portly financier or baronet paired off with a courtesan, and Lady Beatrice was just thinking that she could do with more of this sort of engagement when she heard her name called, in a low voice.

She turned and beheld an old friend of her father's, whom she had once charmed with an hour's sprightly conversation. Lady Beatrice stepped close to him, quickly.

"That is not the name I use now," she said.

"But—my dear child—how could you come to this?"

"Do you truly wish to hear the answer?"

He cast a furtive look around and, taking her by the wrist, led her into an antechamber and shut the door after them, to general laughter from those not too preoccupied to notice.

Lady Beatrice told him her story, in a matter-of-fact way, seated on a divan as he paced and smoked. When she had finished he sank into a chair opposite, shaking his head.

"You deserved better in life, my dear."

"No one deserves good or evil fortune," said Lady Beatrice. "Things simply happen, and one survives them the best one can."

"God! That's true; your father used to say that. He never flinched at unpleasantness. You are very like him, in that sense. He always said you were as true as steel."

Lady Beatrice heard the phrase with a sense of wonder, remembering that long-ago life. It seemed to her, now, as though it had happened to some other girl.

The old friend was regarding her with a strange mixture of compassion and a certain calculation. "For your father's sake, and for your own, I should like to assist you. May I know where you live?"

Lady Beatrice gave him her address readily enough. "Though I do not advise you to visit," she said. "And if you have any gallant ideas about rescuing me, think again. No lady in London would receive me, after what I endured, and you know that as well as I do."

"I know, my dear." He stood and bowed to her. "But women true as steel are found very rarely, after all. It would be shameful to waste your excellent qualities."

"How kind," said Lady Beatrice.

𝒮HE EXPECTED NOTHING from the encounter, and so Lady Beatrice was rather surprised when someone knocked at the door of her lodging three days thereafter.

She was rather more surprised when, upon opening the door, she beheld a blind woman, who asked for her by her name.

"I am she," admitted Lady Beatrice.

"May I come in for a moment, miss, and have a few words with you?"

"As many as you wish," said Lady Beatrice. Swinging her cane before her, the blind woman entered the room. Seemingly quite by chance she encountered a chair and lowered herself into it. Despite her infirmity, she was not a beggar; indeed, she was well-dressed and well-groomed, resembling, if not a lady, certainly someone's respectable mother. Her accents indicated that she had come from the lower classes, but she spoke quietly, with precise diction. She drew off her gloves and bonnet, and held them in her lap, with her cane crooked over one arm.

"Thank you. I'll introduce myself, if I may: Mrs. Elizabeth Corvey. We have a friend in common." She uttered the name of the gentleman who had known Lady Beatrice in her former life.

"Ah," said Lady Beatrice. "And I expect you administer some sort of charity for fallen women?"

Mrs. Corvey chuckled. "I wouldn't say that, miss, no." She turned her goggled face toward Lady Beatrice. The smoked goggles were very black, and quite prominent. "None of the ladies in my establishment require charity. They're quite able to get on in the world. As you seem to be. Your friend told me the sort of things you've seen and done. What's done can't be undone, more's the pity, but there it is.

"That being the case, may I ask you whether you'd consider putting your charms to better use than streetwalking?"

"Do you keep a house of prostitution, madam?"

"I do and I don't," said Mrs. Corvey. "If it was a house of prostitution, you may be sure it would be of the very best sort, with girls as beautiful and clever as you, and some of them as well bred. I am not, myself; I was born in the workhouse.

"When I was five years old they sold me to a pin factory. Little hands are needed for the making of pins, you see, and little keen eyes. Little girls are preferred for the work;

so much more painstaking than little boys, you know. We worked at a long table, cutting up the lengths of wire and filing the points, and hammering the heads flat. We worked by candlelight when it grew dark, and the shop-mistress read to us from the Bible as we worked. I was blind by the age of twelve, but I knew my Scripture, I can tell you.

"And then, of course, there was only one work I was fit for, wasn't there? So I was sold off into a sort of specialty house.

"You meet all kinds of odd ducks in a place like that. Sick fellows, and ugly fellows, and shy fellows. I was got with child twice, and poxed too. I do hope I'm not shocking you, am I? Both of us being women of the world, you see. I lost track of the years, but I think I was seventeen when I got out of there. Should you like to know how I got out?"

"Yes, madam, I should."

"There was this fellow came to see me. He paid specially to have me to himself a whole evening and I thought, *oh, Lord, no*, because you get so weary of it, and the gentlemen don't generally like it if you seem as though you're not paying proper attention, do they? But all this fellow wanted to do was talk.

"He asked me all sorts of questions about myself—how old I was, where had I come from, did I have any family, how did I come to be blind. He told me he belonged to a club of scientific gentlemen. He said they thought they might have a way to cure blindness. If I was willing to let this Gentlemen's Speculative Society try it out on me, he'd buy me out of the house I was in and see that I was physicked for the pox as well, and found an honest living.

"He did warn me I'd lose my eyes. I said I didn't care— they weren't any use anyhow, were they? And he said I might find myself disfigured, and I said I didn't mind that—what had my looks ever gotten me?

"To be brief, I went with him and had it done. And I did lose my eyes, and I was disfigured, but I haven't regretted it a day since."

"You don't appear to be disfigured," said Lady Beatrice. "And clearly they were unable to cure your blindness."

Mrs. Corvey smiled. "Oh, no? The clock says half-past-twelve, and you're wearing such a lovely scarlet dressing-gown, miss, and you have such striking gray eyes—quite unlike mine. You're made of stern stuff, I know, so you won't scream now." Having said that, she slid her goggles up to reveal her eyes.

Lady Beatrice, who had been standing upright, took a step backward and clutched the edge of the table behind her.

"Dear me, you have gone quite pale," said Mrs. Corvey in amusement. "Sets off that scarlet mouth of yours a treat. House of Rimmel Red No. 3, isn't it? Not so pink as their No. 4. And, let me see, why, what a lot of books you have! *Sartor Resartus, Catherine, Falkner*—that's her last one, isn't it?—and, what's that on your bedside table?" The brass optics embedded in Mrs. Corvey's face actually protruded forward, with a faint whirring noise, and swiveled in the direction of Lady Beatrice's bed. "*Nicholas Nickleby.* Yes, I enjoyed that one, myself.

"I do hope I have proven my point now, miss."

"What a horror," said Lady Beatrice faintly.

"Oh, I shouldn't say that at all, miss! My condition is so much improved from my former state that I would go down on my knees and thank God morning and night, if I thought He ever took notice of the likes of me. I have my sight back, after all. I have my health—for I may say the Gentlemen's

Speculative Society has an excellent remedy for the pox—
and agreeable employment. I am here to offer you the
same work."

"Would I pay for it with my eyes?" Lady Beatrice inquired.

"Oh, dear me, no. It would be a crime to spoil *your* looks,
especially when they might be so useful. You were a soldier's
daughter, as I understand it, miss. What would you think of
turning your dishonor into a weapon, in a just cause?

"The Society's very old, you see. In the old days they
had to work secretly, or folk would have burnt them for
witchcraft, with all the astonishing things they invented.
The secrecy was still useful even when times became more
enlightened. There are all manner of devices that make our
lives less wretched, that first came from the Society. They
work to make the world better still.

"Now, it helps them in their work, miss, to have some
sway with ministers and members of Parliament. And who
better controls a man than a pretty girl, eh? A girl with sufficient charm can unlock a man's tongue and find out all sorts
of things the Society needs to know. A girl with sufficient
charm can persuade a man to do all sorts of things he'd never
dream of doing, if he thought anyone else could see.

"And *I* can't see, of course, or so he thinks, for I never
let my secret slip. When a man is a cabinet minister it reas-
sures him to believe that the lady proprietress of his favorite
brothel couldn't identify his face in a court of law. All the
easier for us to trap him later. All the easier to persuade him
to sign a law into being or vote a certain way, which benefits
the Society.

"You and I both know how little it takes to ruin a girl,
when a man can make the same mistakes and the world

smiles indulgently at him. Wouldn't you like to make the world more just?

"You and I both know how little our bodies matter, for all the fuss men make over them. Wouldn't you like to put yours to good use? There are other girls like you—clever girls, well-bred girls. They did one unwise thing, or perhaps, like you, they were unlucky, and the world sent them down to the pavement. But they found they needn't stay there.

"You needn't stay there either, miss. We can offer you a clean, quiet room of your own, with a view of St. James's Park—I never tire of looking at it, myself—and a quiet life, except when working. We need never fear being beaten, or taking ill. We are paid very well. Shall you join us, miss?"

Lady Beatrice considered it.

"I believe I shall," said she.

And she did, to the great relief of the other streetwalkers.

FOUR:

In which she Settles In and learns Useful Things

LADY BEATRICE DISCOVERED that Mrs. Corvey had spoken perfect truth. The house near Birdcage Walk was indeed pleasant, commodious, and adjacent to St. James's Park. Her private room was full of the best air and light to be had in London. It had moreover ample shelves for her books, a capacious wardrobe, and a clean and comfortable bed.

She found her sister residents agreeable as well.

Mrs. Otley was, near Birdcage Walk, a rather studious young lady with fossils she had collected at Lyme Regis and a framed engraving of a scene in Pompeii in her room. At Nell Gwynne's, however, she generally dressed like a jockey, and had moreover a cabinet full of equestrian paraphernalia with which to pander to the tastes of gentlemen who enjoyed being struck with a riding crop while being forced to wear a bit between their teeth.

Miss Rendlesham, though quiet, bespectacled and an enthusiastic gardener, was likewise in the Discipline line, both general and (as needed) specialized. As a rule she dressed in a manner suggesting a schoolmistress, and was an expert at producing the sort of harsh interrogatory tones that made a member of Parliament regress to the age of the schoolroom, where he had been a very naughty boy indeed.

Herbertina Lovelock, on the other hand, was a very good boy, with the appearance of a cupid-faced lad fresh from a public school whereat a number of outré vices were practiced. She wore male attire exclusively, cropped hair pomaded sleek. She also smoked cigars, read the sporting papers with her feet on the fender, and occasionally went to the races. At Nell Gwynne's she had a wardrobe full of military uniforms both Army and Navy, all with very tight trousers with padding sewn into the knees.

The Misses Devere were three sisters, Jane, Dora and Maude, blonde, brunette and auburn-haired respectively. Their work at Nell Gwynne's consisted of unspecialized harlotry and also, when required, group engagements in which they worked as a team.

They alone were forthcoming to Lady Beatrice on the subject of their pasts: it seemed their Papa had been a gentleman, but ruined himself in the customary manner by drinking, gambling and speculating in a joint stock company. Depending on whether one heard the story from Jane, Dora or Maude, their Papa had then either blown his brains out, run away to the Continent with a mistress, or become an opium-smoker in a den in Limehouse and fallen to depths of degradation too appalling to describe. Jane played the pianoforte, Dora played the concertina, and Maude sang. They were equally versatile in other matters.

All ladies resident at the house near Birdcage Walk proved good-natured upon further acquaintance. Lady Beatrice found it pleasant to sit in the common parlour after dinner on Sundays (for Nell Gwynne's did no business on the Sabbath) and attend to her mending while Herbertina read aloud to them all, or the Misses Devere performed a medley of popular songs, as Miss Rendlesham arranged a vase of flowers from the garden. It was agreed that Lady Beatrice ought not alter her scarlet costume in any respect, since it had such a galvanic effect on customers, but Mrs. Corvey and Herbertina went with her to the shops and the dressmaker's to have a few ensembles made up, in rather more respectable colors, for day wear. Mrs. Otley presented her with a small figure of the goddess Athena from her collection of antiquities, for, as she said, "You are so very like her, my dear, with those remarkable eyes!"

All in all, Lady Beatrice thought her new situation most agreeable.

"*O*H, MAJOR, SIR, you wouldn't cane me, would you?" squeaked Herbertina. "Not for such a minor infraction?"

"I'll do worse than cane you, you young devil," leered the Major, or rather the Member of Parliament wearing a major's uniform. He grabbed Herbertina by the arm and dragged her protesting to a plush-upholstered settee. "Drop those breeches and bend over!"

"Oh, Major, sir, must I?"

"That's an order! By God, sir, I'll teach you what obedience means!"

"Look through this eyepiece and adjust the lens until the image comes into focus," said Mrs. Corvey in a low voice, from the adjacent darkened room. Lady Beatrice peered into the camera and beheld the slightly blurry Major gleefully dropping his own breeches.

"How does one adjust it?" Lady Beatrice inquired.

"This ring turns," explained Mrs. Corvey, pointing. Lady Beatrice turned it and immediately the Major came into focus, very much *in flagrante delicto,* with Herbertina looking rather bored as she cried out in boyish horror.

"Now squeeze the bulb," said Mrs. Corvey. Lady Beatrice did so. The gas-jets flared in the room for a moment, but the Major was far too busy to be distracted by the sudden intense brightness, or the faint *click*.

"Have we produced a daguerreotype?" inquired Lady Beatrice, rather intrigued, for she had just been reading about them in a scientific periodical to which Miss Rendlesham subscribed.

"Oh, no, dear; this is a much more advanced process. Something the Society gave us." Mrs. Corvey slid out the plate and slipped in another. "It produces an image that can be printed on paper. That shot was simply for our files. We'll have to wait until he's a bit quieter for an image we can really use. Herbertina will give you the signal."

Lady Beatrice watched carefully as the Major rode to his frenzy and at last collapsed over Herbertina. They ended up reclining on the settee, somewhat scantily clad.

"Now," said the Major, wheezing somewhat, "tell me how enormous I was, and how overpowered you were."

"Oh, Major sir, how could you do such a thing to a young man? I've never felt so helpless," said Herbertina tearfully, making a sign behind her back. Lady Beatrice saw it and squeezed the bulb again. Once more the lamps flared. The Major squinted irritably but paid no further heed, for Herbertina quite held his attention over the next five minutes with her imaginative account of how terrified and submissive the young soldier felt, and how gargantuan were the Major's personal dimensions.

Sadly, neither Mrs. Corvey nor Lady Beatrice heard her inspired improvisations, for they had both retreated to a small room, lit with red de la Rue's lamps and fitted up like a chemist's laboratory. There they had fastened cloth masks over their mouths and noses and were busily developing the plates.

"Oh, these are very good," said Mrs. Corvey approvingly. "Upon my soul, dear, you have a talent for photography."

"Are they to be used for blackmail?"

"Beg pardon? Oh, no; which is to say, only if it should become necessary. And if it should, this one—" she held up the second photograph, with the Major lying on the settee— "can be copied over onto a daguerreotype, and presented as an inducement to cooperate. For the present, the pictures will go into his file. We keep a file, you see, on each of the customers. So useful, when business is brisk, to have a record of each gentleman's likes and dislikes."

"I expect it is indeed. When does it become necessary to blackmail, if I may ask?"

"Why, when the Society requires it. I must say, it isn't necessary often. They're quite persuasive on their own account, and seldom have to resort to such extreme measures. Still, one never knows." Mrs. Corvey hung the prints up to dry. She turned the lever that switched off the de la Rue's lamp and they left the room, carefully shutting the door behind them. The two women walked out into the hidden corridor that ran between the private chambers. From the rooms to either side of the corridor could be heard roars of passion, or pleading cries, and now and again the rhythmic swish and crack of a birch rod over ardent confessions of wickedness.

"Are all of the customers men of rank?" Lady Beatrice inquired, raising her voice slightly to be heard over a baritone bawling *Yes, yes, I did steal the pies!*

"Yes, as a rule; though now and again we treat members of the Society. The fellows whose business it is to go out and manage the Society's affairs, mostly; the rank and file, if you like. They want their pleasures as much as the next man, and most of them have to work a good deal harder to earn them, so we oblige. That is rather a different matter, however, from servicing statesmen and the like.

"In fact, there's rather a charming custom—at least I find it so—of treating the new fellows, before they're first sent on the Society's business. Give them a bit of joy before they go out traveling, poor things, because now and again they do fall in the line of duty. So sad."

"Is it dangerous work?"

"It can be." Mrs. Corvey gave a vague wave of her hand.

They entered the private chamber that served as Mrs. Corvey's office, stepping through the sliding panel and closing it just as Violet, the maid-of-all-work, entered from the reception area beyond.

"If you please, Mrs. Corvey, Mr. Felmouth's just stepped out of the Ascending Room this minute to pay a call. He's got his case with him."

"He'll want his tea, then. How nice! I was hoping we'd be allotted a few new toys." Mrs. Corvey lifted a device from her desk, a sort of speaking-tube of brass and black wax, and after a moment spoke into it: "Tea, please, with a tray of savories. The reception room. Thank you."

She set the device down. Lady Beatrice regarded it with quiet wonder. "And that would be another invention from the Society?"

"Only made by them; it was one of our own ladies invented it. Miss Gleason. Since retired to a nice little cottage in Scotland on the bonus, I am pleased to say. Sends us a dozen grouse every Christmas. Now, come with me, dear, and I'll introduce you to Mr. Felmouth. Such an obliging man!"

FIVE:

In which Ingenious Devices are introduced

THE RECEPTION ROOM was rather larger than a private parlor, with fine old dark paneling on the walls and a thick carpet. It was lit by more de la Rue's lamps, glowing steadily behind tinted shades of glass. A middle-aged gentleman had already removed his coat and hat and hung them up, and rolled up his shirtsleeves; he was perched on the edge of a divan, leaning down to rummage in an open valise, but he jumped to his feet as they entered.

"Mr. Felmouth," said Mrs. Corvey, extending her hand.

"Mrs. Corvey!" Mr. Felmouth bowed and, taking her hand, kissed it.

"And may I introduce our latest sister? Lady Beatrice. Lady Beatrice, Mr. Felmouth, from the Society. Mr. Felmouth is one of the Society's artificers."

"How do you do, sir?"

"Enchanted to make your acquaintance, Ma'am," Mr. Fel-mouth said, stammering rather. He coughed, blushed, and tugged self-consciously at his rolled-up sleeves. "I do hope you'll excuse the liberty, my dear—one gets so caught up in one's work."

"Pray, be seated," said Mrs. Corvey, gliding to her own chair. At that moment a chime rang and a hitherto concealed door in the paneling opened. A pair of respectably clad parlormaids bore in the tea things and arranged them on a table by Mrs. Corvey's chair before exiting again through the same door. Tea was served, accompanied by polite conversation on trivial matters, though the whole time Mr. Felmouth's glance kept wandering from Lady Beatrice to the floor, and hence to his open valise, and then on to Mrs. Corvey.

At last he set his cup and saucer to one side. "Delightful refreshment. My compliments to your staff, Ma'am. Now, I must inquire—how are the present optics suiting you, my dear?"

"Very well," said Mrs. Corvey. "I particularly enjoy the telescoping feature. It's quite useful at the seaside, though of course one must take care not to be noticed."

"Of course. And the implant continues comfortable? No irritation?"

"None nowadays, Mr. Felmouth."

"Very good. Happy to hear it." Mr. Felmouth rubbed his hands together. "However, I have been experimenting with an improvement or two...may I demonstrate?"

"By all means, Mr. Felmouth."

At once he delved into his valise and brought up a leather-bound box about the size of a spectacle case. He opened it with a flourish. Lady Beatrice saw a set of optics very similar to those revealed when Mrs. Corvey had removed her goggles, as she did now. Lady Beatrice involuntarily looked away, then looked back as Mr. Felmouth presented the case to Mrs. Corvey.

"You will observe, Ma'am, that these are a good deal lighter. Mr. Stubblefield in Fabrication discovered a new alloy," said Mr. Felmouth, unrolling a case of small tools. Mrs. Corvey's optics extended outward with a whirr as she examined the new apparatus.

"Yes indeed, Mr. Felmouth, they are lighter. And seem more complicated."

"Ah! That is because...if I may..." Mr. Felmouth leaned forward and applied a tiny screwdriver to Mrs. Corvey's present set of optics, losing his train of thought for a moment as he worked carefully. Lady Beatrice found herself unable to watch as the optics were removed. "Because they are greatly improved, or at least that is my hope. Now then...my apologies, Ma'am, the blindness is entirely temporary...I will just fasten in the new set, and I think you will be pleased with the result."

Lady Beatrice made herself look up, and saw Mrs. Corvey patiently enduring having a new set of optics installed in her living face.

"There," said Mrs. Corvey, "I can see again."

"Splendid," said Mr. Felmouth, tightening the last screw. He sat back. "I trust you find them comfortable?"

"Quite," said Mrs. Corvey, turning her face from side to side. "Oh!" Her optics telescoped outward, a full two inches farther than the range of the previous set, and the whirring sound they produced was much quieter. "Oh, yes, greatly improved!"

"It was my thought that if you held your hands up to obscure them at full extension, you could give anyone observing you the impression that you are looking through a pair of opera glasses," said Mr. Felmouth. "However, permit me to demonstrate the *real* improvement."

He rose to his feet and, going to the nearest lamp, extinguished it by turning a key at its base. He did this with each of the lamps in turn. When he had extinguished the last lamp the room was plunged into Stygian blackness. His voice came out of the darkness:

"Now, Ma'am, if you will give the left-hand lens casing a three-quarter-turn..."

Lady Beatrice heard a faint *click*, and then a cry of delight from Mrs. Corvey.

"Why, the room is quite light! Though everything appears green. Ought it?"

"That is the effect of the filter," said Mr. Felmouth in satisfaction, as he switched on the lamp again. "But it was, I think, bright enough to read by? Yes, that was what I'd hoped for. We will improve it, of course, but from this moment I may confidently assert that you need never endure another moment of darkness, if you are not so inclined."

"How very useful this should prove," said Mrs. Corvey, in satisfaction. "My compliments, Mr. Felmouth! And please extend my thanks to the other kind gentlemen in Fabrication."

"Of course. As it happens, I do have one or two other small items," said Mr. Felmouth, as he went from one lamp to another, switching them back on. He sat down once more and, reaching into his bag, drew out what appeared to be a locket. "Here we are!"

He held it up for their inspection. "Now, ladies, wouldn't you say that was a perfectly ordinary ornament?" Lady Beatrice leaned close to see it; Mrs. Corvey merely extended her optics.

"I should have said so, yes," said Lady Beatrice. Mr. Felmouth raised his index finger, revealing the small hole in the locket's side, with a smaller protrusion a half-inch below.

"No indeed, ladies. This is, rather, positively the last word in miniaturization. Behold." He opened it to reveal a tiny portrait. "And—" Mr. Felmouth thumbed a catch and the portrait swung up, to display a compartment beyond, in which were a minute steel barrel and spring mechanism. "A pistol! The trigger is this knob just below the muzzle. Hold it *so*—aim and fire. Though for best results I recommend firing point-blank, if at all possible."

"Ingenious, I must say," said Mrs. Corvey. To Lady Beatrice she added, a little apologetically, "We do find ourselves in need of self-defense, now and then, you see."

"But surely the bullet must be too small to do much harm," said Lady Beatrice.

"You might think so," said Mr. Felmouth. He brought up an ammunition case, no bigger than a pillbox, and opened it to reveal a dozen tiny pin cartridges ranged in a rack, with a pair of tweezers for loading. "No bigger than flies, are they? However—one point three seconds after lodging in the target, they explode. Not with a quarter of the force of a Guy Fawkes squib, but should the bullet happened to be lodged in the brain or heart at the time, that would be quite enough to drop an assailant in his tracks."

"I would fire into my assailant's ear," said Lady Beatrice thoughtfully. "The entrance wound would be undetectable, and anyone looking at him would suppose the man had died of a stroke."

Mrs. Corvey and Mr. Felmouth stared at her. "I see you are not disposed to be squeamish, dear," said Mrs. Corvey at last. "You'll do very well."

The Misses Devere came wandering sadly into the reception area, dressed in costumes representing a doll, Puss in

Boots and a harlequin respectively. "Our four o'clock gentle-man sent word to say he is unavoidably detained and can't come until tomorrow," said Jane, "and we can't get the catch on the back of Dora's costume unfastened. Lady Beatrice, will you see what you can do? Oh! Hello, Mr. Felmouth!" Jane skipped across the room and sat on his knee. "Have you brought us any toys, Father Christmas?"

Mr. Felmouth, who had gone quite scarlet, sputtered a moment before managing to say "Er—yes, as it happens, I do have one or two more items. H'em! If you'll permit me…" He pulled the bag up on his other knee and took out a couple of the pasteboard cards of buttons generally to be found at notions shops. There were approximately a dozen buttons on each card. One set resembled oystershell pearl buttons; the others appeared to be amber glass.

"The very thing for unruly customers," Mr. Felmouth said, waving the pearl buttons. "Sew them onto a garment, and they appear indistinguishable from ordinary buttons. They are, however, a profoundly strong sedative in a hard sugar shell. You have only to drop one of these in a glass of port wine, or indeed any beverage, and within seconds the button will dissolve. Any gentleman imbibing a wineglassful will fall into a profound sleep within minutes."

"And the amber buttons?" inquired Lady Beatrice, who had risen and was unworking the catch on the back of the Puss in Boots costume.

"Ah! *These* are really useful. One button, dissolved in a man's drink, will induce a state of talkative idiocy. Gently questioned, he will tell you anything, everything. Not all of it will be truthful, I suspect, but I am confident in your powers of discernment. When the drug wears off he will have absolutely no memory of the episode." Mr. Felmouth presented the cards to Mrs. Corvey.

"Splendid," said Mrs. Corvey.

"Oh, won't the amber ones look lovely on my yellow satin?" cried Dora, popping out of the top of her costume as Lady Beatrice freed her hair from the catch. Mr. Felmouth coughed and averted his eyes.

"They would, dear, but they really ought to go to Miss Rendlesham. She would make the best use of them, after all," said Mrs. Corvey. Dora pouted.

"Dear Mr. Felmouth, can't you make up some more in different colors? Miss Rendlesham never wears yellow." Dora leaned close and tickled Mr. Felmouth under his chin with her paw-gloved hand. "Please, Mr. Felmouth? Pussy will catch you a nice fish."

"It, er, ought to be quite easy," said Mr. Felmouth, breathing a little heavily. "Yes, I'm sure I should find nothing easier. Rely on me, ladies."

"As ever, Mr. Felmouth," said Mrs. Corvey.

SIX:

In which Disquieting Intelligence is conveyed

SIR RICHARD H. was of advanced years, quite stout, and so he preferred to lie on his back and engage the angels of bliss, as he called them, astraddle. He lay now groaning with happiness as Lady Beatrice rode away, her gray gaze fixed on the brass rail of the bed, her red mouth curved in a professional smile in which there was something faintly mocking. Her mind was some distance off, wondering how *The Luck of Barry Lyndon* was going to turn out, for she had not yet seen a copy of the latest *Fraser's Magazine*.

At some point her musings were interrupted by the realization that Sir Richard had stopped moving. Lady Beatrice's mind consented to return to the vicinity of her flesh long enough to determine that Sir Richard was, in fact, still alive, if drenched with sweat and puffing like a railway engine. "Are you quite all right, my dear?" she inquired. Sir Richard nodded feebly. She swung herself off him and down, lithe as though he were a particularly well-upholstered vaulting horse, and checked his pulse nevertheless. Having determined that he was unlikely to expire in the immediate future, Lady Beatrice gave him a brief, brisk sponging off with eau de cologne. He was snoring by the time she drew the blanket up over him and went off to bathe in the adjacent chamber.

Lady Beatrice tended her own body with the same businesslike impartiality. During her bout with Sir Richard, her nether regions might have been made of cotton batting like a doll's, for all the sensation she had derived from the act. Even now there was only a minor soreness from chafing. Applying lotion, she marveled once again at the absurd fuss everyone made, swooning over flesh, fearing it, dreading it, lusting after it, when none of it really mattered at all…

She knew there had been a time when the sight of Sir Richard's naked body with its purple tool would have caused her to scream in maidenly dismay; now the poor old thing seemed no more lewd or horrid than a broken-down cart horse. And what had her handsome suitors been but so many splendid racing animals, until they lay blue and stiff in a mountain gorge, when they were even less? They might have had shining souls that ascended to Heaven; it was certainly comforting to imagine so. *Bodies* in general, however, being so impermanent, were scarcely worth distressing oneself.

Lady Beatrice got dressed and returned to the boudoir, where she settled into an armchair and retrieved a copy of *Oliver Twist* from its depths. She read quietly until Sir Richard woke with a start, in the midst of a snore. Sitting up, he asked foggily where his trousers were. Lady Beatrice set her book aside and helped him dress himself, after which she took his arm and escorted him out to the reception area, where he toddled off into the ascending room without so much as a backward glance at her.

"He might have said 'thank you'," observed Mrs. Corvey, from her chair by the tea-table.

"A little befuddled this evening, I think," said Lady Beatrice, leaning down to adjust her stocking. "Have I anyone else scheduled tonight?"

"No, dear. Mrs. Otley is entertaining his lordship until midnight; then we may all go home to our beds."

"Oh, good. May I ask a favor? Will you remind me to look for the latest number of *Fraser's* tomorrow? The last installment—" Lady Beatrice broke off, and Mrs. Corvey turned her head, for both had heard the distinct chime that indicated the ascending room was coming back down with a passenger.

"How curious," said Mrs. Corvey. "Generally the dining area closes at ten o'clock."

"I'll take him," said Lady Beatrice, assuming her professional smile and seating herself on the divan.

"Would you, dear? Miss Rendlesham had such a lot of cleaning up to do, after the duke left, that I gave her the rest of the evening off. You're very kind."

"It is no trouble," Lady Beatrice assured her. The panel slid open and a gentleman emerged. He was bespectacled and balding, with the look of a senior bank clerk, and in fact carried a file case under his arm. He swept his gaze past Lady Beatrice, with no more than a perfunctory nod, focusing his attention on Mrs. Corvey.

"Ma'am," he said.

"Mr. Greene?" Mrs. Corvey rose to her feet. "What an unexpected pleasure, sir. And what, may one ask, is *your* pleasure?"

"Not here on my own account," said Mr. Greene, going a little red. "Though, er, of course I should like to have the leisure to visit soon. Informally. You know. Hem. In any case, Ma'am, may we withdraw to your office? There is a matter I wish to discuss."

"Of course," said Mrs. Corvey.

"I don't mind sitting up. Shall I watch for any late guests?" Lady Beatrice inquired of Mrs. Corvey. Mr. Greene turned and looked at her again, more closely now.

"Ah. The new member. I knew your father, my dear. Please, join us. I think perhaps you ought to hear what I have to say as well."

Mr. Green, having accepted a cup of cocoa in the inner office, drank, set it aside and cleared his throat.

"I don't suppose either of you has ever met Lord Basmond?"

"No indeed," said Mrs. Corvey.

"Nor have I," said Lady Beatrice.

"Quite an old family. Estate in Hertfordshire. Present Lord, Arthur Rawdon, is twenty-six. Last of the line. Unmarried, did nothing much at Cambridge, lived in town until two years ago, when he returned to the family home and proceeded to borrow immense sums of money. Hasn't gambled; hasn't been spending it on a mistress; hasn't invested it. Has given out that he's making improvements on Basmond Hall, though why such inordinate amounts of rare earths should be required in home repair, to say nothing of such bulk quantities of some rather peculiar chemicals, is a mystery.

"There were workmen on the property, housed there, and they won't talk and they can't be bribed to. The old gardener does visit the local public house, and was overheard to make disgruntled remarks about his lordship destroying the yew maze, but on being approached, declined to speak further on the subject."

"What does it signify, Mr. Greene?" said Mrs. Corvey.

"What indeed? The whole business came to our attention when he purchased the rare earths and chemicals; for, you know, we have men who watch the traffic in certain sorts of goods. When an individual exceeds a certain amount in purchases, we want to know the reason why. Makes us uneasy.

"We set a man on it, of course. His reports indicate that Lord Basmond, despite his poor showing at university, nevertheless seems to have turned inventor. Seems to have made some sort of extraordinary discovery. Seems to have decided to keep it relatively secret. And most certainly *has* sent invitations to four millionaires, three of them foreign nationals I might add, inviting them to a private auction at Basmond Park."

"He intends to sell it, then," said Lady Beatrice. "Whatever it is. And imagines he can get a great deal of money for it."

"Indeed, miss," said Mr. Greene. "The latest report from our man is somewhat overdue; that, and the news of this auction (which came to us from another source) have us sufficiently alarmed to take steps. Fortunately, Lord Basmond has given us an opportunity. It will, however, require a certain amount of, ah, immoral behavior."

"And so you have come to us," said Mrs. Corvey, with a wry smile.

"It will also require bravery. And quick wits," Mr. Greene added, coloring slightly. "Lord Basmond sent out a request to a well-known establishment for a party of four, er, girls to supply entertainment for his guests. We intercepted the request. We require four volunteers from amongst your ladies here, Mrs. Corvey, to send to the affair."

"And what are we to do, other than service millionaires?" asked Lady Beatrice. Mr. Greene coughed.

"You understand, it is strictly voluntary—but we want to know what sort of invention could fetch a price only a millionaire could pay. Is it, for example, something that touches on our national security? And we need to know what has become of the man we got inside."

"We shall be happy to oblige," said Mrs. Corvey, with a graceful wave of her hand.

"We would be profoundly grateful, Ma'am." Mr. Greene stood and bowed, offering her the file case. "All particulars are here. Communication on the usual frequency. I shall leave the matter in your capable hands, Ma'am."

He turned to depart, and abruptly turned back. Very red in the face now, he took Lady Beatrice's hand and, after a fumbling moment of indecision, shook it awkwardly.

"God bless you, my dear," he blurted. "First to volunteer. You do your father credit." He fled for the reception chamber, and a moment later they heard him departing in the ascending room.

"Am I to assume there are certain dangers we may face?" said Lady Beatrice.

"Of course, dear," said Mrs. Corvey, who had opened the file case and was examining the documents within. "But then, what whore does not endure hazards?"

"And do we do this sort of work very often?"

"We do." Mrs. Corvey looked up at her, smiling slightly. "We are no *common* whores, dear."

SEVEN:

In which Visitors arrive at Basmond Hall

As THE VILLAGE of Little Basmond was some distance from the nearest railway line, they took a hired coach into Hertfordshire. Mrs. Corvey sat wedged into a corner of the coach, studying the papers in the file case, as the Devere sisters chattered about every conceivable subject. Lady Beatrice gazed out the window at the rolling hills, green even in winter, unlike any that she had ever known. The streets of London were a realm out of nature, easy to learn, since one city is in its essentials like any other; but the land was another matter. Lady Beatrice found it all lovely, in its greenness, in the vastness of the tracts of woodland with their austere gray branches; but her senses were still attuned to a hotter, dryer, brighter place. She wondered whether she would come in time to grow accustomed to—she very nearly said *Home* to herself, and then concluded that the word had lost any real meaning.

"...but it was only fifty-four inches wide, and so I was obliged to buy fifteen yards rather than what the pattern called for—" Jane was saying, when Mrs. Corvey cleared her throat. All fell silent at once, looking at her expectantly.

"Arthur Charles Fitzhugh Rawdon," she said, and drew out a slip of pasteboard the size of a playing card. Lady Beatrice leaned forward to peer at it. It appeared to be a copy of a daguerreotype. Its subject, holding his lapels and looking self-important, stood beside a Roman column against a painted backdrop of Pompeii. Lord Basmond was slender and pale, with small regular features and eyes of liquid brilliance; Lady Beatrice had thought him handsome, but for the fact that his eyes were set somewhat close together.

"Our host," said Mrs. Corvey. "Or our employer, if you like; one or all of you may be required to do him."

"What a pretty fellow!" said Maude.

"He looks bad-tempered, though," observed Dora.

"And I am quite sure all of you are practiced enough in the art of being agreeable to avoid provoking him," said Mrs. Corvey. "Your work will be to discover what, precisely, is being auctioned at this affair. We may be fortunate enough to have it spoken of in our presence, with no more thought of our understanding than if we were dogs. *He* may be more discreet, and in that case you will need to get it out of the guests. I suspect the lot of you will be handed around like bonbons, but if any one of them takes any one of you to his bedroom, then I strongly recommend the use of one of Mr. Felmouth's nostrums."

"Oh, jolly good," said Dora in a pleased voice, lifting the edge of her traveling cloak to admire the amber buttons on her yellow satin gown.

"Our other objective…" Mrs. Corvey sorted through the case and drew out a second photograph. "William Reginald

Ludbridge." She held up the image. The subject of the portrait faced square ahead, staring into the camera's lens. He was a man of perhaps forty-five, with blunt pugnacious features rendered slightly diabolical by a moustache and goatee. His gaze was shrewd and leonine.

"One of our brothers in the Society," said Mrs. Corvey. "The gentleman sent to Basmond Park before us, in the guise of a laborer. He seems to have gone missing. We are to find him, if possible, and render any assistance we may. I expect that will be my primary concern, while you lot concentrate on the other gentlemen."

At that moment the coach slowed and, shortly, stopped. The coachman descended and opened the door. "The Basmond Arms, ladies," he informed them, offering his arm to Mrs. Corvey.

"Mamma, the kind man has put out his arm for you," said Maude. Mrs. Corvey pretended to grope, located the coachman's arm and allowed herself to be helped down from the coach.

"So very kind!" she murmured, and stood there feeling about in her purse while the other ladies were assisted into Basmond High Street, and their trunks lifted down. Temporarily anonymous and respectable, they stood all together outside the Basmond Arms, regarded with mild interest by passers-by. At length the publican ventured out and inquired whether he might be of service.

"Thank you, good man, but his lordship is sending a carriage to meet us," said Mrs. Corvey, just as Jane pointed and cried, "Oooh, look at the lovely barouche!" The publican, having by this time noticed their paint and the general style of their attire, narrowed his eyes and stepped back.

"Party for the Hall?" inquired the grinning driver. He pulled up before the public house. "Scramble up, girls!"

Muttering, the publican turned and went back indoors as the ladies approached the carriage. The driver jumped down, loaded on their trunks and sprang back into his seat. "How about the redhead sits beside me?" said the driver, with a leer.

"How about you give us a hand up like a gentleman, duckie?" retorted Maude.

"Say no more." The driver obliged by giving them each rather more than a hand up, after which Maude obligingly settled beside him and submitted herself to a kiss, a series of pinches and a brief covert exploration of her ankle. Lady Beatrice, observing this, fingered her pistol-locket thoughtfully, but Maude seemed equal to defending herself.

"Naughty boy!" said Maude, giving the driver an openly intimate fondle in return. The driver blushed and sat straight. He shook the reins and the carriage moved off along the high street, running a gauntlet of disgusted looks from such townsfolk as happened to be lounging on their front steps or leaning over their garden walls.

"My gracious, they ain't quite a friendly lot here, are they?" Maude inquired pertly, in rather coarser accents than was her wont. "Doesn't his lordship have working girls to call very often?"

"You're the first," said the driver, who had recovered a little of his composure. Looking over his shoulder to be certain they had passed the last of the houses, he slipped his arm around Maude's waist.

"The first! And here we thought he was a right sporting buck, didn't we, girls? What's your name, by-the-bye?"

"Ralph, miss—I mean—my dear."

"Well, you're a handsome chap, Ralph, and I'm sure we'll get on." Maude leaned into his arm. "So his lordship ain't a bit of an exquisite, I hope? Seems a bit funny him hiring us on if he is."

Ralph guffawed. "Not from what I heard. He ain't no sporting buck, but he did get a girl with child when he was at Cambridge. Sent her back here to wait it out, but the little thing died in any case."

"What, the girl?"

"No! The baby. It wasn't right. His lordship's been more careful since, I reckon."

"Well, what's he want with us, then?" Maude reached up and stroked Ralph's cheek, tracing a line with her fingertip down to his collar. "A big stout man like you, I know *you* know what to do with a girl. His lordship don't fancy funny games?"

"I reckon you're for his party," said Ralph, shivering. "For the guests."

"Oooh! We likes parties, girls, don't we?" Maude looked over her shoulder. As she looked back Ralph grabbed her chin and gave her a violent kiss of some length, until Jane was obliged to tell him rather sharply to mind the horse.

"It's all right," said Maude, surfacing for air with a gasp. "Look here, girls, I've taken such a fancy to our dear friend Ralph, would you ever mind very much if we pulled up a moment?"

"Please yourself," said Mrs. Corvey. The carriage happened to be proceeding down a long private drive along an aisle of trees at that moment, and Ralph steered the carriage to one side before taking Maude's hand and leaping down. They disappeared into the shrubbery. Lady Beatrice looked at Mrs. Corvey and raised an eyebrow in inquiry. Mrs. Corvey shrugged. "Helps to have friends and allies, doesn't it?" she said.

"Is that Basmond Hall?" Dora stood and peered up the aisle at a gray bulk of masonry just visible on a low hill beyond rhododendrons. Mrs. Corvey glanced once toward the shrubbery and, removing her goggles a moment, extended her optics for a closer look at the building.

"That would be it," she said, replacing her goggles. "Historic place. Dates back to the Normans and such."

"An old family, then," said Lady Beatrice.

"And his lordship the last of them," said Mrs. Corvey. "Interesting, isn't it? I do wonder what sort of fellow he is."

In due course Maude and Ralph emerged from the bushes, rather breathless. Ralph swept Maude up on the seat with markedly more gallantry than before, jumping up beside her bright-eyed.

"Had a nice rattle, did you?" inquired Mrs. Corvey. Ralph ducked his head sheepishly, but Maude patted his arm in a proprietary way.

"He's a jolly big chap, dear Ralph is. But we shan't mention our little tumble to his lordship, shall we? Wouldn't want you to lose your place, Ralph dear."

"No, ma'am," said Ralph. "Very kind of you, I'm sure."

They proceeded up the drive and beheld Basmond Hall in all its gloomy splendor. If Lord Basmond had given home improvement as his reason for borrowing money, it was certainly a plausible excuse; for the Hall was an ancient motte and bailey of flints, half-buried under a thick growth of ivy. No Tudor-era Rawdons had enlarged it with half-timbering and windows; no Georgian Rawdons had given it any Palladian grace or statues. Nor did it seem now that the Rawdon of the present age had any intention of making the place over into respectable Gothic Revival; there was no sign that so much as a few pounds had been spent to repoint the masonry.

Ralph drove the carriage up the slope, over the crumbling causeway that had replaced the drawbridge, and so under the portcullis into the courtyard.

"How positively medieval," observed Dora.

"And a bit awkward to get out of, if one had to," murmured Mrs. Corvey under her breath. "Caution is called for, ladies."

Lady Beatrice nodded. It all looked like an illustration from one of her schoolbooks, or perhaps *Ivanhoe*; the courtyard scattered with straw, the stables under the lowering wall, the covered well, the Hall with its steep-pitched roof and the squat castle behind it. All it wanted was a churl polishing armor on a bench.

Instead, a black-suited butler emerged from the great front door and gestured frantically at Ralph. "Take them to the trade entrance!"

Ralph shrugged and drove the wagon around to a small door at the rear of the Hall. Here he stopped and helped the ladies down as grandly as any knight-errant, while the butler popped out of the trade door and stood there wringing his hands in detestation.

"Here you go, Pilkins," said Ralph. "Fresh-delivered roses!"

Pilkins shooed them inside and they found themselves in the back-entryway to the kitchens, amid crates of wines and delicacies ordered from some of the finest shops in London. Some two or three parlormaids were peering around a door frame at them, only to be ordered away in a hoarse bawl by the cook, who came and stared.

"I never thought I'd see the day," she said, shaking her head grimly. "Common whores in Lord Basmond's very house!"

"I beg your pardon," said Mrs. Corvey, tapping her cane sharply on the flagstones. "Very high-priced *and* quality whores, ordered special, and my girls would be obliged to you for a nice cup of tea after such a long journey, I'm sure."

"Fetch them something, Mrs. Duncan," said Pilkins. Pursing his mouth, he turned to Mrs. Corvey. "I assume you are their...proprietress, madam?"

"That's right," said Mrs. Corvey. "And am in charge of their finances as well. We was promised a goodly sum for this occasion, and I'm sure his lordship won't be so mean as to renege."

"His lordship will, in fact, be here presently to see whether your—your girls—are satisfactory," said Pilkins, his elocution a little hampered by the difficulty he had unpursing his lips.

"Of course they're satisfactory! Girls, drop your cloaks," said Mrs. Corvey.

They obeyed her. The plain gray traveling gear fell away to reveal the ladies in all their finery. Lady Beatrice wore her customary scarlet, and the Devere sisters had affected jewel tones: Maude in emerald green, Jane in royal blue, and Dora in golden yellow satin. The effect of such voluptuous color in such a drab chamber was breathtaking and a little barbaric. Pilkins, for one, found himself recalling certain verses of Scripture. To his horror, he became aware that his manhood was asserting itself.

"If that ain't what his lordship ordered, I'm sure I don't know what is," said Mrs. Corvey. Pilkins was unable to reply, for several reasons that need not be given here, and in the poignant silence that followed they heard footsteps hurrying down the stairs and along the corridor.

"Are those the whores?" cried an impatient voice. Arthur Rawdon, Lord Basmond, entered the room.

"None other," said Mrs. Corvey. Lord Basmond halted involuntarily, with a gasp of astonishment upon seeing them.

"By God! I'm getting my money's worth, at least!"

"I should hope so. My girls are very much in demand, you know," said Mrs. Corvey. "And they don't do the commoner sort of customer."

"Ah." Lord Basmond gawked at her. "Blind. And you would be their…"

"Procuress, my lord."

"Yes." Lord Basmond rubbed his hands together as he walked slowly round the ladies, who obligingly struck attitudes of refined invitation. "Yes, well. They're not poxed, I hope?"

"If you was at all familiar with my establishment, sir, you would know how baseless any allegations of the sort must be," said Mrs. Corvey. "Only look, my lord! Bloom of youth, pink of health, and not so much as a crablouse between the four of 'em."

"We'd be happy to give his lordship a closer look at the goods," said Dora, fingering her buttons suggestively. "What about a nice roll between the sheets before tea, dear, eh?" But Lord Basmond backed away from her.

"No! No thank you. Y-you must be fresh for my guests. Have they been told about the banquet?"

"Not yet, my lord," said Pilkins, blotting sweat from his face with a handkerchief.

"Well, tell them! Get them into their costumes and rehearse them! The business must proceed perfectly, do you understand?"

"Yes, my lord."

"And where are my girls to lodge, your lordship?" Mrs. Corvey inquired. Lord Basmond, who had turned as though to depart, halted with an air of astonishment.

"Lodge? Er—I assume they will lie with the guests."

"I ain't, however," said Mrs. Corvey. "And do require a decent place to sleep and wash, you know."

"I suppose so," said Lord Basmond. "Well then. Hem. We'll just have a bed made up for you in...erm..." He turned his back on the ladies and gestured wildly at Pilkins, mouthing in silence *The closet behind the stables,* and pointed across the yard to be sure Pilkins got the point. "A nice little room below the coachman's, quite cozy."

"How very kind," said Mrs. Corvey.

But the window looks out on the—mouthed Pilkins, with an alarmed gesture. Lord Basmond grimaced and, with his index finger, drew Xs in the air before his eyes.

She won't see anything, you idiot, he mouthed. Pilkins looked affronted, but subsided.

"Certainly, my lord. I'll have Daisy see to it at once," he replied.

"See that you do." Lord Basmond turned and strode from the room.

EIGHT:

In which Proper Historical Costuming is discussed

THEY WERE GRUDGINGLY served tea in the pantry, and then ushered into another low dark room wherein were a great number of florist's boxes and a neatly folded stack of bedsheets.

"Those are your costumes," said Pilkins, with a sniff.

"Rather too modest, aren't they?" remarked Lady Beatrice. "Or not modest enough. What are we intended to do with them?"

Pilkins studied the floor. "His lordship wishes you to fashion them into, er, togas. The entertainment planned is to resemble, as closely as possible, a—hem—bacchanal of the ancient Romans. And he wishes you to resemble, ah, nymphs dressed in togas."

"But the toga was worn by men," Lady Beatrice informed him. Pilkins looked up, panic-stricken, and gently Lady Beatrice pressed on: "I suspect that what his lordship requires is the chiton, as worn by the ancient hetaerae."

"If you say so," stammered Pilkins. "With laurel wreaths and all."

"But the laurel wreath was rather worn by—"

"Bless your heart, dear, if his lordship wishes the girls to wear laurel wreaths on their heads, I'm sure they shall," said Mrs. Corvey. "And what must they do, besides the obvious? Dance, or something?"

"In fact, they are to bear in the dessert," said Pilkins, resorting to his handkerchief once more. "Rather a large and elaborate refreshment on a pallet between two poles. And if they could somehow contrive to dance whilst bringing it in, his lordship would prefer it."

"We'll do our best, ducks," said Maude dubiously.

"And there are some finger-cymbals in that red morocco case, and his lordship wishes that they might be played upon as you enter."

"In addition to dancing and carrying in the dessert," said Lady Beatrice.

"Perhaps you might practice," said Pilkins. "It is now half-past noon and the dinner will be served at eight o'clock precisely."

"Never you fear," said Mrs. Corvey. "My girls is nothing if not versatile."

At that moment they heard the sound of a coach entering the courtyard. "The first of the guests," exclaimed Pilkins, and bolted for the door, where he halted and called back "Sort out the costumes for yourselves, please," before closing the door on them.

"Nice," said Mrs. Corvey. "Jane, dear, just open the window for us?"

Jane turned and obliged, exerting herself somewhat to pull the swollen wood of the casement free. The light so admitted was not much improved, for the window was tiny and blocked by a great deal of ivy. "Shall I try to pull a few leaves?" Jane asked.

"Not necessary, dear." Mrs. Corvey stepped close to the window and, removing her goggles, extended her optics through the cover of the vines.

"What do you see?"

"I expect this is the Russian," said Mrs. Corvey. "At least, that's a Russian crest on his coach. Prince Nakhimov, that was the name. Mother was Prussian; inherited businesses from her and invested, and it's made him very rich indeed. Well! And there he is."

"What's he look like?" asked Maude.

"He's quite large," said Mrs. Corvey. "Has a beard. Well dressed. Footman, coachman, valet. There they go—he's been let off at the front door, I expect. Well, and who's this? Another carriage! Ah, now that must be the Turk. Ali Pasha."

"Oh! Has he got a turban on?"

"No, dear, one of those red sugar-loaf hats. And a military uniform with a lot of ornament. Some sort of official that's made a fortune in the Sultan's service."

"Has he got a carriage full of wives?"

"If he had, I should hardly think he'd bring them to a party of this sort. No, same as the other fellow: footman, driver, valet. And here's the next one! This would be the Frenchman, now. Count de Mortain, the brief said; I expect that's his coat-of-arms. Millionaire like the others, because his family did some favors for Bonaparte, but mostly the wealth's in his land. A bit cash-poor. Wonder if Lord Basmond knows?

"And here's the last one. Sir George Spiggott. No question *he's* a millionaire; pots of money from mills in the north.

Bad-tempered looking man, I must say. Well, ladies, one for each of you; and I doubt you'll get to choose."

"I suppose Lord Basmond is a bit of a fairy prince after all," said Maude.

"Might be, I suppose." Mrs. Corvey turned away from the window. "Notwithstanding, if he *does* require your services in the customary way, any one of you, be sure to oblige and see if you can't slip him something to make him talkative into the bargain."

*H*AVING BEEN LEFT to fend for themselves, the ladies spent an hour or two devising chitons out of the bed sheets. Fortunately Jane had a sewing kit in her reticule, and found moreover a spool of ten yards of peacock blue grosgrain ribbon in the bottom of her trunk, so a certain amount of tailoring was possible. The florist's boxes proved to contain laurel leaves indeed, but also maidenhair fern and pink rosebuds, and Lady Beatrice was therefore able to produce chaplets that better suited her sense of historical accuracy.

They were chatting pleasantly about the plot of Dickens' latest literary effort when Mrs. Duncan opened the door and peered in at them.

"I don't suppose one of you girls would consider doing a bit of honest work," she said.

"Really, madam, how much more honest could our profession be?" said Lady Beatrice. "We dissemble about nothing."

"What's the job?" inquired Mrs. Corvey.

Mrs. Duncan grimaced. "Churning the ice cream. The swan mold arrived by special post this morning, and it's three times the size we thought it was to be, and the girls and I have about broke our arms trying to make enough ice cream to fill the damned thing."

"As it's in aid of the general entertainment for which we was engaged, my girls will be happy to assist at no extra charge," said Mrs. Corvey. "Our Maude does a lot of heavy lifting and is quite strong, ain't you, dear?"

"Yes, Ma'am," replied Maude, dropping a curtsey. Mrs. Duncan, with hope dawning in her face, ventured further:

"And, er, if some of you wouldn't mind—there's some smallwork with the sugar paste, and the jellied Cupids want a steady hand in turning out…"

$\mathcal{A}$PRONS WERE FOUND for them and the ladies ventured forth to assist with the Dessert.

A grain-sack carrier had been set across a pair of trestles, with a vast pewter tray fastened atop it, and a massive edifice of cake set atop that. One of the maids was on a stepladder, crouched over the cake with a piping-bag full of icing, attempting to decorate it with a frieze of scallop shells. As they entered, she dropped the bag and burst into tears.

"Oh! There's another one crooked! Oh, I'll lose my place for certain! Mrs. Duncan, I ain't no pastry cook, and my arm hurts like anything. Why don't I just go out and drown myself?"

"No need for theatrics," said Lady Beatrice, taking up the piping-bag. "Ladies? Forward!"

There was, it seemed, a great deal more to be done on the Dessert. There was sugar paste to press into pastillage forms to make all manner of decorations, including a miniature Roman temple, doves, a chariot, and bows and arrows. There were indeed Cupids of rose-flavored jelly to be turned out of their molds, resulting in rather horrible-looking little things like pinkly transparent babies. They wobbled, heads drooping disconcertingly as real infants, once mounted at the four corners of the cake. There were pots and pots of muscadine-flavored cream to be poured into the sorbetiere and churned, with grinding effort, before scraping it into the capacious hollow of an immense swan mold. When it was filled at last it took both Maude and Dora to lift it into the ice locker.

"And that goes on top of the cake?" Lady Beatrice asked.

"It's supposed to," said Mrs. Duncan plaintively, avoiding her gaze.

"And we're to carry that in and dance too, are we?" said Jane, pointing with her thumb at the main mass of the Dessert, which was now creaking on its supports with the weight of all the temples, Cupids, doves and other decorations, to say nothing of the roses and ferns trimming its bearer-poles.

"Well, that was what his lordship said," Mrs. Duncan replied. "And I'm sure you're all healthy young girls, ain't you? And it ain't like he ain't paying you handsome."

NINE:

In which the Object of Particular Interest appears

ANY FURTHER CONCERNS were stilled, a half-hour into the dinner service, when Pilkins and Ralph entered the kitchen, bearing between them an object swathed in sacking. Ralph stopped short, gaping at the ladies in their chitons, and Pilkins swore as the object they carried fell to the kitchen flagstones with a clatter. Lady Beatrice glimpsed the corner of a long flat box like a silverware case, before Pilkins hurriedly covered it over again with the sacking.

"You great oaf! Mind what you're about," said Pilkins. "And you, you—girls, clear out of here. You too, Cook. Go wait in the pantry until I call."

"Well, I like that! This ain't your kitchen, you know," cried Mrs. Duncan.

"Lordship's orders," said Pilkins. "And you can go with them, Ralph."

"Happy to oblige," said Ralph, sidling up to Maude.

"If you please," said Mrs. Corvey, "My rheumatism is painful, now that night's drawn on, and I find it troublesome to move. Mightn't I just bide here by the fire?"

Pilkins glanced at her. "I don't suppose *you'll* matter. Very well, stay there; but into the pantry with the rest of you, and be quick about it."

The ladies obeyed, with good grace, and Mrs. Duncan with markedly less enthusiasm. Ralph stepped after them and pulled the door shut.

"Heigh-ho! 'Here I stand like the Turk, with his doxies around,'" he chortled. "Saving your presence, Cook," he added, but she slapped him anyway.

Mrs. Corvey, meanwhile, watched with interest as Pilkins unwrapped the box—rather heavier, apparently, than its appearance indicated—and grunted with effort as he slid it across the floor to the creaking trestle that supported the Dessert. Mrs. Corvey saw what appeared to be a row of dials and levers along its nearer edge.

Pilkins pushed it underneath the trestle and fumbled with it a moment. Mrs. Corvey heard a faint humming sound, then saw the box rise abruptly through the air, as though it fell *upward*. It struck the underside of the tray with a crash and remained there, apparently, while Pilkins crouched on the flagstones and massaged his wrists, muttering to himself.

Then, almost imperceptively at first but with increasing violence, the Dessert began to tremble. The jellied Cupids shook their heads, as though in disbelief. As Mrs. Corvey watched in astonishment, the Dessert on its carrier lifted free of the trestles and rose jerkily through the air. It was within a hand's breadth of the ceiling when Pilkins, having exclaimed an oath and scrambled to his feet, reached up frantically and made some sort of adjustment with the dials and levers. One end of the carrier dipped, then the other; the whole affair leveled itself, like a new-launched ship, and settled gently down until it bobbed no more than an inch above its former resting place on the trestles. The flat box was so well screened by drooping ferns and flowers as to be quite invisible.

Pilkins sagged onto a stool and drew a flask from his pocket.

"Are you quite all right, Mr. Pilkins?" said Mrs. Corvey.

"Well enough," said Pilkins, taking a drink and tucking the flask away.

"I only wondered because I heard you lord mayoring there, in a temper."

"None of your concern if I was."

"I reckon his lordship must be a trial to work for, sometimes," said Mrs. Corvey, in the meekest possible voice. Pilkins glared at her sidelong.

"An old family, the Rawdons. If they've got strange ways about them, it's not my place to talk about 'em with folk from outside."

"Well, I'm sure I meant no harm—" began Mrs. Corvey, as Mrs. Duncan threw the pantry door open with a crash.

"I'll see you get your notice, Ralph, you mark my words!" she cried. "I ain't staying in there with him another minute. He's a fornicating disgrace!"

"Indeed, I think he does a very creditable job." Maude's voice drifted from the depths of the pantry. Ralph emerged from the pantry smirking, followed by the ladies. Upon seeing the floating Dessert, Ralph pointed and exclaimed:

"Hi! That's what it does, is it? I been going mad wondering—"

Mrs. Duncan, noticing the Dessert's new state, gave a little scream and backed away. "Marry! He's done it again, hasn't he? That unnatural—"

"Hold your noise!" Pilkins told her.

"Whatever's the matter?" said Mrs. Corvey.

"The Dessert appears to be levitating," Lady Beatrice said.

"Oh, stuff and nonsense! I'm sure it's just a conjuror's trick," said Mrs. Corvey. Pilkins gave her a shrewd look.

"That's it, to be sure; nothing but a stage trick, as his lordship likes to impress people."

"So the Dessert isn't really floating in midair?" Jane poked one of the Cupids with a fingertip, causing it to writhe. "Just as you say; I'm only grateful we shan't kill ourselves carrying it in."

A bell rang then. Pilkins jumped to his feet. "That's his lordship signaling for the next course! Get those finger cymbals on, you lot! Where's the bloody swan?"

The swan was heaved out in its mold and upended over the cake, and a screw turned to let air into its vacuum; the swan unmolded and plopped into its place on the cake with an audible thud, sending the Cupids into quivering agonies.

"Right! Pick the damned thing up! He wants you *smiling* and, and exercising your wiles when you go out there!" cried Pilkins.

"We strive to please, sir," said Lady Beatrice, taking her place on one of the carrier poles. The Devere sisters took their places as well. They found that the Dessert lifted quite easily, for it now seemed to weigh scarcely more than a few ounces. Lady Beatrice struck up a rhythm on the finger cymbals, the Devere sisters cut a few experimental capers, and Pilkins ran before them up the stairs and so to the vast banqueting table of Basmond Hall.

"I could do with a dram of gin, after all that," said Mrs. Duncan, collapsing into her chair.

"I could too," said Ralph.

"Well, you can just take yourself off to the stables!"

"Perhaps you'd be so kind as to guide me to my room?" asked Mrs. Corvey. "I'm rather tired."

TEN:

In which a Proposition is Advanced

LORD BASMOND HAD spared no expense in the pursuit of his chosen *motif*; an oilcloth had been laid down over the flagstones and painted with a design resembling tiled mosaic on a villa floor. Hothouse palms had been carried about and placed in decorative profusion, as had an abundance of aspidistra. Five chaise-lounges had been set around the great central table on which Lady Beatrice spied the remains of the grand dishes that had preceded the Dessert from the kitchen: A roast suckling pig, a roast peacock with decorative tail, a dish of ortolans, a mullet in orange and lemon sauce.

On the chaise-lounges reclined Lord Basmond and his four guests. The gentlemen were flushed, all, with repletion. Lord Basmond, alone pale and sweating, sat up as the ladies entered and flung out an arm.

"*Now*, sirs! For your amusement, I present these lovely nymphs bearing a delectable and mysterious treat. The nymphs, being pagan spirits, have absolutely no morals what-soever and will happily entertain your attentions in every respect. As for the other treat...you may have heard of a dish called 'Floating Island'. That is a mere metaphor. Behold the substance! Nymphs, free yourselves of your burden!"

Lady Beatrice let go her corner of the Dessert and essayed a Bacchic dance, drawing on her memories of India. She glimpsed Maude and Dora pirouetting and Jane perform-ing something resembling a frenzied polka, finger-cymbals clanging madly. Alas, all terpsichorean efforts were going unnoticed, for the banqueters had riveted their stares on the Dessert, which drifted gently some four feet above the oil-cloth. Lord Basmond, having assured himself that all was as he had intended, turned his gaze on the faces of his guests, and hungrily sought to interpret their expressions. Lady Beatrice considered them, one after the other.

Prince Nakhimov had lurched upright into a sitting posi-tion, gaping at the unexpected vision, and now began to laugh and applaud. Ali Pasha had glanced once at the Dessert, was distracted by Jane's breasts (which had emerged from the top of her chiton like rabbits bounding from a fox's den) and then, as what he had seen registered in his mind, turned his head back to the Dessert so sharply he was in danger of dislocating his neck.

Count de Mortain watched keenly and got to his feet, seemingly with the intention of going closer to the Dessert to see what the trick might be. He got as far as the end of his chaise-lounge before Dora leapt into his arms—her rib-bons and securing stitches had all come unfastened, with results that had been catastrophic, were the party of another sort—and they plumped down together on the lounge. The

Count applied himself to an energetic appreciation of Dora's charms, but continued to steal glances at the Dessert. Sir George Spiggott's mouth was wide in an O of surprise, his eyes round too, but there was a scowl beginning to form.

"What d'you call this, then—" he exclaimed, ending in a *whoof* as Maude jumped astride him and emulated a few of Lady Beatrice's movements.

"What do I call it?" replied Lord Basmond, in rather a theatrical voice. "A demonstration, gentlemen. Here I come to the point and purpose of your presences here. All of you are men of means and influence; you would know whether your respective governments would be interested in a discovery so momentous it may grant ultimate power to its owner."

"What do you mean?" demanded Sir George, who had got his breath back, as he peered around Maude. Lord Basmond cleared his throat and struck an attitude.

"When I was at Cambridge, gentlemen, I studied the vanished civilization of Egypt. I chanced to be taking a holiday in France when I was approached by an elderly beggar, a former member of the late emperor's army and a veteran of the Egyptian campaign. In his destitution he was obliged to offer for sale certain papyrus scrolls he had looted, from what source he was unable to recall, in the land of the pharaohs.

"I purchased the scrolls and returned with them to England. When they yielded up their secrets to translation, I was astonished to discover therein the method by which the very pyramids themselves were built! The ancient priests had developed a means of circumventing the force of gravity itself, gentlemen, and not with charms or spells but by the application of sound scientific principles! Vast blocks of stone were made to float, as light as balloons. Sadly, the scrolls were later lost in a fire, but fortunately not before I had committed their texts to memory.

"Consider the confection floating before you. Do you see any wires? Any props? You do not, because there are none. I have been able to reproduce the device used by the Egyptians, and I intend to sell my secret to the highest bidder.

"Now, consider the applications! Any nation owning my device must swiftly outpace its rivals for dominance. Think of the speed and ease in public works, when a single workman may lift slabs of stone as though they were feathers. Think of the industrial uses to which this may be put, gentlemen. And—dare I say it—the uses for national defense? Envision cannons or supply wagons that might be floated with the ease of soap bubbles and the speed of sleds. Imagine floating platforms from which enemy positions may be spied out, or even fired upon.

"And he who offers the highest bid gains this splendid advantage, gentlemen!"

"What is your reserve?" inquired Prince Nakhimov.

"Two million pounds, sir," replied Lord Basmond, as Sir George uttered an oath.

"You ought to have offered it to your own countrymen first, you swine!"

"You were invited, weren't you? If you want it, you're free to outbid the others," said Lord Basmond coolly. "But, please! I perceive the ice cream is melting. Let us enjoy our treat, and hope that its effects will sweeten your temper. Pleasure before business, gentlemen; tomorrow you will be given a tour of my laboratory and witness further astonishing demonstrations of levitation. Bidding will commence at precisely two in the afternoon. Tonight, you will enjoy my hospitality and the ministrations of these charming females. Pilkins? Serve the sweet course, please."

"At once, sir," said Pilkins, climbing onto a chair.

An orgy commenced.

ELEVEN:

*In which our Heroine and her Benefactress
Make Discoveries*

HAVING BID RALPH a civil good-night, Mrs. Corvey edged past her trunk and seated herself on the narrow bed that had been made up for her. Her hearing was rather acute, an advantage gained from the years of her darkness, and so she listened patiently as Ralph climbed the creaking stairs that led to his room above the stables. He undressed himself, he climbed into bed, he indulged in a prolonged episode of onanism (if Mrs. Corvey was any judge of the audible indicators of male solitary passion) and, finally, he snored.

When she was assured Ralph was unlikely to wake, Mrs. Corvey rose and walked to the end of her room, where a single small window admitted the light of the moon. She looked out and beheld a view down the steep slope to the gardens behind Basmond Hall. Perhaps *garden* was an ambitious term; there appeared to be an old orchard and a few rows of cabbages and herbs, on the near edge of a vast overgrown park. Directly below, however, was a modern structure of brick and slate, perhaps twice the size of a coachhouse, and in sharp contrast to the general air of picturesque ruin characteristic of Basmond Hall.

Mrs. Corvey regarded it thoughtfully a moment, before turning from the window and opening her trunk. She undressed quickly and drew forth a boy's clothing, simple dark trousers and a knitted jersey. Donning this attire, she opened a hidden panel in the trunk's lid and revealed a box containing a dozen brass shells, roughly the size of rifle ammunition. Taking her cane, she made certain alterations to it and loaded the shells into the chamber revealed thereby. So prepared, Mrs. Corvey crept from her room and into the courtyard, keeping to the shadows along its eastern edge.

It somewhat discomfited her to discover that the portcullis had been lowered. A moment's study of the grate, however, revealed that its iron gridwork had been constructed to block the entrance of great-thewed knights of old. Mrs. Corvey, by contrast, being female and considerably undernourished in her younger years, was sufficiently small enough to writhe through without much difficulty. She scrambled down the hillside and into the dry moat, and so made her way around to the gardens.

There she stepped out upon a short space of level lawn, somewhat ill-cared-for. Beyond it was the new structure, built close against the hillside. Mrs. Corvey wondered briefly whether it might be a hothouse, for the north face was almost entirely windows. Circling around it, she was surprised to note no door in evidence, nor did the windows appear to open.

Mrs. Corvey removed her goggles and extended her optics against the glass. Moonlight was illuminating the building's interior clearly. She saw no plants of any kind; rather, several tables upon which were glass vessels of the sort associated with chemists' laboratories. Upon other tables were tools and small machinery, at the purpose of which she could only speculate. The dark bulk of a steam engine crouched in one corner. In the other corner Mrs. Corvey spotted a door, and realized that the only entrance to the laboratory was from within; for the door was in the wall that backed up to the hill behind, and must communicate with a tunnel beyond that led upward into the tower above.

Nodding to herself, Mrs. Corvey proceeded to study the leading around the window panes. Near the ground she found a spot in which the pane had, apparently, been recently replaced, for the lead solder was brighter there. Drawing a long pin from her hair, she busied herself for a few minutes prizing down the lead, and after diligent work slipped out the glass and set it carefully to one side. Crawling through the gap thereby created was no more difficult than going through the portcullis had been; indeed, Mrs. Corvey mused to herself that she might have made a first-rate burglar, had fate decreed other than her present situation.

For the next while she examined the laboratory at some length, committing its details to memory and wishing that Mr. Felmouth would exert himself to build a camera small enough to be carried on such occasions. In vain she looked for any notes, papers or journals that might illuminate the purpose of the machines. At last Mrs. Corvey addressed the door with her hairpin, and a long moment later stood gazing into the utter darkness of the tunnel on the other side.

IN RETROSPECT, LADY Beatrice was obliged to admit that bedsheets made an admirably practical costume for the evening's festivities. In the course of her employment she had become liberally smeared with ice cream, sugar icing, cake crumbs, rose petals and spilled wine. The last item had fountained over her breasts, not in an excess of Bacchic enthusiasm, but when Prince Nakhimov had been startled into dropping his glass by the sight of Sir George swallowing one of the jellied Cupids whole. ("The damned press claim I eat workers' babies for breakfast," Sir George had said smugly. "Let's see if I can open my jaws wide enough!")

Lady Beatrice serviced each of the guests in turn during the amusements, for they were, one and all, inclined to share the ladies' favors. Lord Rawdon unbent so far as to permit himself to be fellatiated, when his guests insisted he partake of the carnal blisses available, but declined to retire with anyone when the long evening drew to its close. Rather, Lady Beatrice found herself claimed by Prince Nakhimov; Ali Pasha took Dora off to his bed. Jane was taken, in a brisk and businesslike manner, by Sir George Spiggott, and Maude retired on the arm of Count de Mortain.

In the privacy of the bedchamber Prince Nakhimov divested himself of his garments, and proved to be a veritable Russian Bear for hairiness and animal spirits. The sheer athleticism required left Lady Beatrice somewhat fatigued, and therefore she was more than a little discountenanced when, after two hours of his attentions, the prince pulled the blankets up, rolled away from her, and said: "Thank you. You may go now."

"But am I not to sleep here?"

"*Shto*?" The prince looked over his shoulder at her, surprised. "Sleep here? You? I never sleep with, please pardon my frankness, whores." He turned back toward his pillow and Lady Beatrice, profoundly irritated, picked up the sticky remnants of her costume and held it against herself as she left his room.

She faced now the choice of wandering downstairs in her present state of undress and searching for her trunk, there to change into a robe, and afterward to seek repose on one of the chaise-lounges in the dining room until morning, or simply opening one of the other bedroom doors and seeing if any of the other couples had room in bed for a third party. Being desirous of sleep, Lady Beatrice opted for the chaise-lounge.

She descended the stairs and made her way along the gallery that led to the grand staircase. Strong moonlight slanted in through the windows at this hour, throwing patches of brilliant illumination on several of the portraits that hung along the walls. Lady Beatrice slowed to examine them. It was plain that Lord Basmond was a true Rawdon; here in face after face were the same lustrous eyes and delicate features, to say nothing of a certain chilly hauteur common to all the portraits' subjects. Lady Beatrice remarked particularly one painting, upon which the moonlight fell directly. It was of a child, she supposed, a miniature beauty in Elizabethan costume. The wide lace collar framed the heart-shaped face. A silver net bound the hair, so fair as to appear white, and the contrast of the dark eyes with such ethereal pallor was striking indeed. *Hellspeth Rawdon, Lady Basmond,* read the brass plate on the lower frame.

Lady Beatrice, conscious of the cold, walked on. She had passed the last of the portraits when she spied a door ajar, through which the corner of a bed could be glimpsed. Hopeful of finding a warmer resting place for the night, Lady Beatrice opened the door and peered within.

The room was feebly lit by a single candle, much reduced in height, beside the bed. Lord Basmond lay across the bed, still fully dressed. His eyes were open and glistening in the candle-light. Lady Beatrice saw at once that he was dead. Nonetheless, she stepped across the threshold and had a closer look.

His mouth was open in a silent cry of protest. No wounds were in evidence; rather the unnatural angle of his neck told plainly what had effected Lord Basmond's dispatch. He can have been dead no more than two hours, and yet in that time seemed to have shrunken within his evening clothes. He looked frail and pathetic. Lady Beatrice thought of the ancestral portraits, all the centuries fallen down to this sad creature lying sprawled and broken, last of the long line.

Lady Beatrice swept the room with a glance, looking for obvious clues, but found none. She stepped back into the corridor and stood pensive a moment, considering what she ought to do next.

TWELVE:

In which Still More Discoveries are made

LADY BEATRICE DECIDED fairly quickly that nothing much could be accomplished in her present state of undress, and therefore she went down to the kitchen. The fire there was banked, the range still radiating pleasant warmth, and so she pumped a few gallons of water and heated them sufficiently to bathe herself by the hearth.

Having located her trunk, she dressed herself in the fire-light and went out by the side door, making her way across the courtyard to the stables. She found the room that had been assigned to Mrs. Corvey and knocked softly, intending to report her discovery. When no reply came to her knock she opened the door and saw the empty bed. Returning to the kitchens, Lady Beatrice encountered Dora, just coming down the stairs in a state of sticky nudity, trailing what remained of her costume.

"Oh, good, the fire's lit," Dora exclaimed, tossing aside her costume and going to the sink to pump water. "If I don't bathe I shall simply scream. Did yours snore too?"

"No; he pitched me out."

"Ah! They do, sometimes, don't they? My pasha went at it like a stoat in rut until he fell asleep, and then he snored so loud the bed curtains trembled."

"You never got a chance to drug him, then?"

"What, with my little buttons? No. In the first place he wouldn't drink any wine, and anyway, what would have been the point of drugging him? *We* know as much as *he* does. If we want to find out any more about the levitation device, the one to drug would be Lord Basmond."

"That would be rather difficult now, I'm afraid," said Lady Beatrice, and told what she had found on entering his lordship's bedchamber. Dora's eyes widened.

"No! You're sure?"

"I know a dead man when I see one," said Lady Beatrice.

"Damn and blast! *So* convenient to murder someone when there are whores about to blame for it. I suppose now we'll have to run all screaming and hysterical to the butler and report it. Jane and Maude will have firm alibis, at least. First, however, we'll need to report to the missus." Dora set a bucket of water on the fire.

"She isn't in her room," explained Lady Beatrice.

"No? I suppose it's possible *she* did for his lordship."

"Would she?"

"You never know; I should think it was a bit treason-ous, wouldn't you, offering an invention like that to other empires? She may have made the decision to do for him and confiscate the thing for the Society. If she did, she may be out making arrangements to cover our tracks."

"Let's not go running to Pilkins yet, then," said Lady Beatrice. "What became of the rest of the Dessert?"

"That's a good question," said Dora. "Pantry?"

They left the silent kitchen and, following a trail of cake crumbs and blobs of crème anglaise, located the remaining Dessert in the pantry, as expected. Thoroughly ruined now, it lay spilt sideways on the flagstones, its grain carrier leaning against the wall.

"Once more, damn and blast," said Dora. "Where's the marvelous flying thing? The box or plank or whatever it was Pilkins carried in?"

"Not here, at any rate," said Lady Beatrice.

"You don't suppose the missus took it?"

"Might have, but—" Lady Beatrice began, as a prolonged bumping crash came from above. They looked at each other and ran upstairs, Lady Beatrice lifting her skirts to hurry. Dora, being nimbler in her present state of undress, arrived in the great hall first. Lady Beatrice heard her exclaim a fairly shocking oath, and upon joining her discovered why; for Arthur Fitzhugh Rawdon, Lord Basmond, lay in a crumpled heap at the foot of the great staircase.

The two ladies stood there considering his corpse for a long moment.

"Frightfully convenient accident," said Lady Beatrice at last.

"I think it will look better if you do the screaming," said Dora, with a gesture indicating her nudity.

"Very well," said Lady Beatrice. Dora retreated to the kitchen. Lady Beatrice cleared her throat and, drawing a deep breath, uttered the piercing shriek of a terrified female.

Mrs. Corvey paused only to switch on the night-vision feature of her optics before advancing down the tunnel. Instantly she beheld the tunnel walls and floor, stretching ahead into a green obscurity. She had expected the same neat brickwork that distinguished the laboratory building, but the tunnel appeared to be of some antiquity: haphazardly mortared with flints, here and there buttressed with timbers, and penetrated with roots throughout, threadlike white ones or gnarled and black subterranean limbs.

As she proceeded along the tunnel's length, Mrs. Corvey noted in several places the print of shoes. Most were small, not much bigger than her own, but twice she saw a much larger track, a man's certainly. Moreover she perceived strange and shifting currents of air in the tunnel. About a hundred yards in she spotted what must be their source, for a second tunnel opened where some of the flint and mortar had fallen in, creating a narrow gap in the wall.

Mrs. Corvey studied the tunnel floor in front of the gap. Someone had gone through in the recent past, to judge from the way the earth was disturbed. She turned and considered the main course of the tunnel, which ended a few yards ahead where a ladder ascended, doubtless to the tower above. Yielding to her intuition, however, she turned back and slipped through the gap into the second tunnel.

Here the walls seemed of greater antiquity still, indeed, scarcely as though shaped by human labors at all; rather burrowed by some great animal. There was an earthy damp smell and, distantly echoing, the sound of trickling water. Mrs. Corvey peered into the depths and spotted something scarlet ahead in the green gloom, an irregular mass against one wall.

She lifted her cane to her shoulder and went forward cautiously, five feet, ten feet, and then there was a sudden burst of hectic illumination and a blare of—sound? No, not sound; Mrs. Corvey was at a loss to say what sensation it was that affected her nerves so painfully. She swayed for a moment before regaining her balance. Two or three deep breaths restored her composure before she heard a groan in the darkness ahead. And then:

"You know," said a male voice, "if I'm to die here I'd much rather be shot. All this blinding me and chaining me to walls and so forth is becoming tedious."

THIRTEEN:

In which Mr. Ludbridge tells a Curious Story

THE SCARLET MASS had shifted, and resolved itself now into the shape of a man, slumped against the wall of the tunnel with one arm flung up awkwardly. As she neared him, Mrs. Corvey saw that he was in fact pinioned in place by a manacle whose chain had been passed about one of the ancient roots.

"Mr. Ludbridge?" she inquired.

His head came up sharply and he turned his face in her direction.

"Is that a lady?"

"I am, sir. William Reginald Ludbridge?"

"Might be," he said. She was within a few paces of him now and, opening a compartment in her cane, drew forth a lucifer and struck it for his benefit. The circle of dancing light so produced proved to her satisfaction that the prisoner was indeed the missing man Ludbridge. "Who's that?"

"I am Elizabeth Corvey, Mr. Ludbridge. From Nell Gwynne's."

"Are you? What becomes of illusions?"

"We dispel them," she replied, relieved to remember the countersign, for she was seldom required to give it.

"And we are everywhere. If you're wondering why your match isn't producing any light, it's because of that damned—excuse me—that device you tripped just now. It'll be at least an hour before we can see anything again."

"In fact, I can see now, Mr. Ludbridge." She blew out the tiny flame.

"I beg your pardon? Oh! *Mrs.* Corvey. You're the lady with the...do forgive me, madam, but I hardly expected the GSS to send the ladies' auxiliary to my aid. So the flash hasn't affected your, er, eyes?"

"It does not appear to have, sir."

"That's something, anyway. Er...I trust you weren't sent alone?"

"I was not, sir. Some of my girls are upstairs, I suppose you'd say, entertaining Lord Basmond and his guests."

"Ha! Ingenious. I don't suppose you happen to have a hacksaw with you, Mrs. Corvey?"

"No, sir, but let me try what I might do with a bullet." Mrs. Corvey set the end of her cane against the root where the manacle's chain passed over it, and pressed the triggering mechanism. With a *bang* the chain parted, and white flakes of root drifted down like snow. Ludbridge's arm fell, a dead weight.

"I am much obliged to you," said Ludbridge, gasping as he attempted to massage life back into the limb. "What have you found out?"

"We know about the levitation device."

"Good, but that isn't all. Not by a long way. There's this thing in the tunnel that makes such an effective burglar-catcher, and I suspect there's more still."

"What precisely is it, Mr. Ludbridge?"

"Damned if I know, beg your pardon. You saw the laboratory, did you?"

"Indeed, Mr. Ludbridge, I entered that way."

"So did I. Crawled through and had a good look round. Took notes and made sketches, which I still have here somewhere..." Ludbridge felt about inside his coat. "Yes, to be sure. Had started up the other tunnel when I heard the trap opening above and someone starting down the ladder. Put out my light in a hurry and ducked into what I'd assumed was an alcove in the wall, hoping to avoid notice. Bloody thing crumbled backward under my weight and I fell in here.

"I heard quick footsteps hurry past, in the main tunnel without. When I felt safe I lit my candle again and looked around me. This place is only the entrance to a great network of tunnels, you know, quite a warren; it's a wonder Basmond Hall hasn't sunk into the hill. I could hear water and felt the rush of air, so I thought I'd explore and see if I could find myself a discreet exit.

"That was two weeks ago, I think. I never found an exit, though I did find a great deal else, some of it very queer indeed. There's a spring-fed subterranean lake, ma'am, and what looks to be some of the ancestral tombs of the Rawdons— at least, I hope that's what they are. Midden heaps full of rather strange things. Someone lived in this place long before the Rawdons came with William the Conqueror, I can tell you that! I'm ashamed to admit I became lost more than once. If not for the spring and my field rations I'd have died down there.

"Having found my way back up at last, I was proceeding in triumph down this passageway when I ran slap into the—the whatever-it-is that makes such a flash-bang. I was knocked unconscious the first time. When I woke I discovered I'd been chained up as you found me. That was…yesterday? Not very clear on the passage of time, I'm afraid."

"Clearly Lord Basmond had noticed someone was trespassing," said Mrs. Corvey.

"Too right. Haven't seen him, though. He hasn't even come down to gloat, which honestly I'd have welcomed; always the chance I could persuade him to join the GSS, after all. Just as well it was you, perhaps."

"And what are we to do now, Mr. Ludbridge?"

"What indeed? I am entirely at your disposal, ma'am."

Mrs. Corvey turned and looked intently at the floor of the tunnel. She saw, now, the braided wire laid across their path, and the metal box to which it was anchored.

"I think we had better escape, Mr. Ludbridge."

FOURTEEN:

*In which Lord Basmond is mourned,
with Apparent Sincerity*

H E MUST HAVE fallen," declared Sir George Spiggott.

"A lamentable accident," said Ali Pasha, looking very hard at Sir George. So did Jane, who had trailed after them clutching her chiton to herself.

"What becomes of the auction now, may I ask?" said Prince Nakhimov.

"He had bones like sugar-sticks," said Pilkins through his tears. He was on his knees beside Lord Basmond's body. "Always did. Broke his arm three times when he was a boy. Oh, Lord help us, what are we to do? He was the only one with...I mean to say..."

"The only one with the plans for the levitation device?" said Lady Beatrice. Pilkins looked up at her, startled, and then his face darkened with anger.

"That's enough of your bold tongue," he shouted. "I'm not having the constable see you lot here! I want you downstairs, all of you whores, now! Get down there and keep still, if you know what's good for you!" He turned to glare at Dora, who had just come up in a state of respectable dress from the kitchens.

"Suit yourself; we'll go," she said. Looking around, she added "But where's Maude?"

"Where is the Count de Mortain? He cannot have slept through such screams," said Prince Nakhimov.

"Perhaps I'd better go fetch her," said Lady Beatrice, starting up the stairs.

"No! I said you were...were to...oh, damned fate," said Pilkins, drooping with fresh tears. "Go on, get up there and wake them up. And then I want to see the back of you all."

"Happy to oblige," said Jane, striding past him to go downstairs. Lady Beatrice, meanwhile, ran up the grand staircase and along the gallery, where the faces of Rawdons past watched her passage. The moonlight had shifted from her portrait, but Hellspeth Rawdon still seemed to glimmer with unearthly luminescence.

Lady Beatrice knocked twice at the door of the bedroom that had been allotted to the Count de Mortain, but received no response. At last, opening the door and peering in, she beheld one candle burning on the dresser and Maude alone in the bed, deeply asleep.

"Maude!" Lady Beatrice hurried in and shook Maude's shoulder. "Wake up! Where is the count?"

Maude remained unconscious, despite Lady Beatrice's best efforts. Lady Beatrice sniffed at the dregs remaining in the wine glass on the bedside table, and thought she detected some medicinal odor. There was no sign of Count de Mortain in the room.

When this fact was communicated to the parties downstairs, Sir George Spiggott exclaimed, "It's the damned frog! I'll wager a thousand pounds *he* pushed Lord Basmond down the stairs!"

"You had better send for your constabulary now, rather than wait for morning," Ali Pasha told Pilkins.

"In the meanwhile, perhaps someone would assist me in getting Maude downstairs?" Lady Beatrice inquired. Prince Nakhimov volunteered and brought Maude, limp as a washrag, down as far as the Great Hall; from there Lady Beatrice and Dora carried her between them down to the kitchen.

"How awfully embarrassing," said Jane, from the hearthrug where she was bathing. "*We* were supposed to be the ones administering drugs!"

"We ought to have expected this," said Lady Beatrice grimly. She went to the sink and pumped a bucketful of cold water. "I should think the count drugged her and then killed Lord Basmond, meaning to steal the device."

"What?" Jane looked up from soaping herself. "I thought his lordship fell down the stairs."

Dora explained that Lady Beatrice had found Lord Basmond dead in his bedroom before his body had been flung down the stairs. Jane's eyes narrowed.

"Don't be so sure the count was his murderer," she said. "Mine was in a towering temper—did me only once, quite rough and nasty, and kept telling me it was a damned good thing I was English. At last he got out of bed and left. I asked him where he was going and he told me to mind my own business. He wasn't gone above ten minutes. When he came back he looked a different man—white and shaking.

I pretended to be asleep, because I was tired of his nonsense, but he didn't try to wake me for any more fun. He tossed and turned for about twenty more minutes and then leaped out of bed and ran from the room. He was only gone about five minutes this time, and very much out of breath when he came back. Jumped into bed and pulled the covers up. It seemed only a moment later we heard you screaming."

"Did he ever seem as though he paused to hide something in the bedroom?" asked Lady Beatrice, upending the bucket's contents over Maude, who groaned and tried to sit up.

"No, never."

"He might have killed his lordship, but that doesn't mean the device has been stolen," said Dora, crouching beside Maude and waving a bottle of smelling salts under her nose. Maude coughed feebly and opened her eyes.

"Damn and blast," she murmured.

"Wake up, dear."

"That bastard slipped me a powder!"

"Yes, dear, we'd guessed."

"And we'd had such a lovely time in bed." Maude leaned forward, massaging her temples. "Such a jolly and amusing man. He's got no money, though. Told me he was delighted to accept a night of free food and copulation, but isn't in any position to bid on the levitation device."

"Have you any idea where he's got to?"

"None. What's been going on?"

The other ladies gave her a brief summary of what had occurred. In the midst of it, Mrs. Duncan came shuffling downstairs in tears, clutching a candlestick.

"Oh, it's too cruel," she sobbed. "What'll become of us now? And the Basmonds! What of the Basmonds?"

"Bugger the Basmonds," said Maude, who was still feeling rather ill.

"How dare you, you chit! They're one of the oldest families in the land!" cried Mrs. Duncan. "Ruined now, ruined! And there he went and spent all the trust fund—What's to happen now?" She sank down on a stool and indulged in furious tears.

"Trust fund?" asked Lady Beatrice.

"None of your bloody business. It's the end of the Basmonds, that's all."

"There aren't any cousins to inherit?" inquired Dora sympathetically.

"No." Mrs. Duncan blew her nose. "And poor Master Arthur never married, on account of him being—well—"

"A fairy prince?" said Jane, toweling herself off. Lady Beatrice winced, for it was hardly a tactful remark, but Mrs. Duncan lifted her head sharply.

"You been reading in the library? You wasn't allowed in there!"

"No, I haven't read anything. I don't know what you mean," said Jane.

"That's in a book in the library," said Mrs. Duncan. "About the Rawdons having fairy blood. Old Sir Robert finding a girl sitting up there on the hill in the moonlight, and she putting a spell on him. And that was why, ever since…" She trailed off into tears again.

"What a charming story," said Lady Beatrice. "Now, if you'll pardon a change of subject, my dear: I notice the levitation device has been removed from under the cake. Do you happen to know where it was put?"

"Wasn't put anywhere," said Mrs. Duncan. "I pushed the nasty thing into the pantry like it was and left it for morning. You mean to say it's gone?"

FIFTEEN:

In which our Heroine is Obliged to Exert Herself

MRS. CORVEY, UPON inspecting the box on the passage floor, discovered a switch on one end. Cautiously, using her cane, she pushed the switch to its opposite position. A humming noise ceased, so faint it had been imperceptible until it stopped.

"I believe we may now pass safely, Mr. Ludbridge."

"Glad to hear it," Ludbridge said, wheezing as he tried to get to his feet. "Oh—ow—oh, bloody hell, I'm half crippled."

"You may lean on me," said Mrs. Corvey, taking his hand and pulling his arm around her shoulders. "Not to worry, dear; I'm a great deal stronger than I look."

"As yet I've no idea what you look like at all," replied Ludbridge. "Ha! The blind leading the blind, although in our case it makes excellent sense. Lead on, dear lady."

They made their way out again into the main tunnel, and hurriedly down it to the laboratory. Ludbridge was able to crawl through the hole in the window easily enough, but was obliged afterward to sit and catch his breath.

"It seems a lifetime ago I went in there," he said, gasping. "By God, the night air smells sweet! Rather odd nobody noticed the pane missing in all that time, though."

"In fact, someone did," said Mrs. Corvey. "It had been replaced when I found it this evening."

"Really? Well, that's enough to lend new vigor to my wasted limbs," said Ludbridge, getting up with a lurch. "Let's get the hell out of here, shall we?"

Mrs. Corvey led him out through the hedge and around the moat. She had a moment of worry about getting through the portcullis, for Ludbridge was a man of respectable girth. However, just as they came to the causeway the portcullis came rattling up. Someone drove the carriage forth in great haste; the portcullis was left open behind them. Mrs. Corvey looked after the carriage in keen interest, thinking she recognized Ralph gripping the reins. She wondered what might have happened, to send him out at such speed.

"We had best hurry, Mr. Ludbridge," she said.

"Swiftly as I may, ma'am," he replied, crawling after her on hands and knees. When they reached the courtyard Mrs. Corvey was disconcerted to see lights blazing in the Great Hall. She endeavored to pull Ludbridge along after her, and was greatly relieved when they tumbled together through the door into her room.

"FORTY YEARS I'VE worked here," said Mrs. Duncan, somewhat indistinctly, for she was now on her third glass of gin. The scullery and parlor maids, all in their nightgowns, were huddled around her like chicks around a hen, in varying degrees of tearful distress.

"Well, consider: you are now at liberty to travel," said Jane helpfully. Mrs. Duncan gave her a dark look and two of the maids were provoked into fresh weeping.

"I've just remembered," said Lady Beatrice. "I left something in Prince Nakhimov's room. I wouldn't wish to be so indiscreet as to take the front stairs, when the constable may arrive any moment...Are there back stairs, Mrs. Duncan?"

The cook pointed at a doorway beyond the pantry. "Mind you be quick about it."

"I shall endeavor to be," said Lady Beatrice. With a significant glance at the Devere sisters, she hastened up the back stairs.

"Lordship's good name at stake and all..." muttered Mrs. Duncan, and had another dram of gin.

*L*ADY BEATRICE RAN at her best speed, and arrived at last in the gallery. She paused a moment, catching her breath, listening. She heard Prince Nakhimov telling a long anecdote, to which Sir George, Pilkins, Ali Pasha and several valets were listening. Creeping to the edge of the grand staircase she beheld them through a fog of cigar smoke, seated around Lord Basmond's corpse.

Turning, she crossed the gallery and went up to the guests' rooms. She opened the count's door and stepped within. The candle still illuminated the room. By its light Lady Beatrice made a quick and thorough search for the levitation device.

Opening the count's trunk, she dug through folded garments. Upon encountering a book she drew it forth and examined it. It was merely a popular novel, but stuck within were a number of papers. One in particular bore an official seal, and appeared to have been signed by Metternich. Lady Beatrice's grasp of French was imperfect, but sufficient for her to make out a phrase here and there. *You will attempt by any means possible to see if his lordship would be agreeable...do not need to remind you of the consequences if you fail...*

"I did not know that whores were fond of reading."

Lady Beatrice looked up. A man stood in the doorway of the antechamber connecting to Count de Mortain's room. His accent was harsh, Germanic; he appeared to be the count's valet. He was holding a knife. Lady Beatrice considered her options, which were few.

"We aren't," she replied. "I was looking for the count; did you know there's been an accident? Lord Basmond is dead."

The valet had started toward her, menace in his eyes, but at her news he stopped in astonishment. "Dead!"

She hurled herself at him and bore him backward. They fell across the bed. The valet stuck at her with the knife. Lady Beatrice experienced then an eerie sense of stepping away from herself, of watching as the patient draft animal of her body bared its teeth and fought for its life. The struggle was a vicious one, as any fight between animals must be. Lady Beatrice was pleased to observe that her flesh had not lost the strength it had drawn upon in the Khyber Pass. She was particularly pleased to see herself wrenching the knife from the valet's hand and stunning him with a sharp downward strike of the pommel. He sagged backward, momentarily unconscious.

So far sheer instinct had preserved her; now Lady Beatrice picked herself up, poured a glass of water from the carafe on the bedside table, and dropped into it a button torn from her blouse. The button dissolved with a gentle hiss. She lifted the valet's head, murmuring to him in a soothing voice, and held the glass to his lips. He drank without thinking, before opening his eyes.

"*Danke, mutter...*" he whispered. He opened his eyes, looked up at Lady Beatrice, and started. "Filthy bitch! I'll kill you—"

"Bitch, unfortunately, yes. Filthy? Certainly not." Lady Beatrice held him down without much effort, as the drug took its swift effect. "And certainly not the sort of bitch who allows herself to be killed by men like you. Yes, you do feel unaccountably sleepy now, don't you? You can barely move. Just close your eyes and go back to Dreamland, dear. It will be so much easier."

When he lay unconscious at last, and having verified by lifting his eyelid that he was, in fact, unconscious, Lady Beatrice rose and considered him coldly. She lifted his legs onto the bed, removed his shoes, and moreover made certain adjustments to his clothing in order to suggest the lewdest possible scenario to anyone discovering him later. Then Lady Beatrice retrieved the papers she had dropped from the floor and secreted them in her bodice.

She left the room and closed the door quietly.

SIXTEEN:

In which a Curious Creature is introduced

"YOU KNOW, I believe my sight has returned," said Ludbridge, blinking and rubbing his eyes. Mrs. Corvey, who had just finished changing her clothing while explaining how matters presently stood, turned to raise an eyebrow at him.

"My congratulations, Mr. Ludbridge. Lovely feeling, isn't it?"

"It is indeed, Mrs. Corvey."

"Now, Mr. Ludbridge, I believe I'll just go see how my ladies are getting on. Like to know why all the lights are burning at the Hall, as well. I suggest you avail yourself of the soap and the washbasin and polish yourself up a bit, eh? So you don't look quite so much as though you'd spent the last fortnight mucking about in caves. There's a hairbrush and a comb on the table you can use, too."

"Thank you, ma'am, I certainly shall."

Mrs. Corvey drew her shawl around her shoulders and stepped out into the courtyard. She walked briskly toward

the Great Hall, watching the lit windows, and consequently
was startled when she trod on something unexpected. She
looked down. She stared for a long moment at what lay in
the courtyard. Then Mrs. Corvey turned around and walked
back to the room behind the stables. She opened the door
and beheld Ludbridge in the act of washing his face. When,
puffing and blowing like a walrus, he reached for a towel,
she said:

"If you please, Mr. Ludbridge, there's a dead Frenchman
outside. I wonder if you would be so kind as to come have a
look at him?"

"Happy to oblige," said Ludbridge, and followed her out
into the courtyard. When they reached the corpse he drew
a small cylindrical object from his pocket and adjusted a
switch on it. A thin beam of brilliant light shot from one end,
occasioning a cry of admiration from Mrs. Corvey.

"Oh, I do hope Mr. Felmouth makes up a few of those
for me!"

"We call them electric candles; very useful. Let's see the
beggar..." Ludbridge shone the light on the dead man's face,
and winced. Count de Mortain's features were still recogniz-
able, for all that they were distorted and frozen in a grimace
of fear; quite literally frozen too, blue with cold, glittering
with frost. His arms were stretched above his head like a
diver's, his fingers crooked as though clawing.

"What the deuce! This is Emile Frochard!"

"Not the Count de Mortain?"

"Not half. This fellow's a spy in the pay of the Austrians!
But they've been blackmailing the real count. Shouldn't be sur-
prised if they hadn't intercepted the invitation to this auction.
Well, well. Damned odd. I wonder how he died?"

"I believe I have an idea," said Mrs. Corvey, glancing it the house. "I'll know more presently."

"Ought we to do anything with him?"

"No! Let him lie for now, Mr. Ludbridge."

$\mathscr{L}$ADY BEATRICE STOOD still a moment in the corridor outside the bedchambers, listening intently. Prince Nakhimov had apparently launched into another anecdote, something to do with hunting wolves. An icy gust of wind crossed the floor, so unexpected as to make Lady Beatrice start. Were she a less ruthlessly pragmatic woman, she had imagined some spectral origin to the chill. A moment's keen examination of the hallway revealed that a tapestry hung at the rear of the hall, moving as though stirred by a breeze. Lady Beatrice glimpsed the bottom of a door in the wall.

She approached it warily and drew the tapestry aside. The revealed door was ajar. Lady Beatrice saw beyond a short corridor, lit by moonlight through unglazed slit-windows, with another door at its end.

Venturing into the corridor, Lady Beatrice peered through one of the windows and saw that it was high in the air, in effect an enclosed bridge connecting the rear of the house with the tower atop the motte. She hurried across bare wooden planks and tried the door at the other end. It opened easily, for the lock was broken.

Lady Beatrice stood blinking a moment in the brilliant light of the room beyond. The light came not from candles or oil lamps, but from something very like an immense battery of de la Rue's vacuum lamps; and this astonished Lady

Beatrice, for, as far as she had been aware, no one but the Gentlemen's Speculative Society had been able to build practical vacuum lamps.

Her astonishment was as nothing, however, compared to that of the room's occupant. He turned, saw her, and froze a moment. He might have been Lord Basmond's ghost, so like him he was; but smaller, paler, infinitely more fragile-looking. His hands and naked feet were white as chalk, and too long to seem graceful. In the way of clothing he wore only trousers with braces and a shirt, cuffs rolled up prodigiously, and a leather band about his nearly hairless head. Clipped to the band were several pairs of spectacles of different sorts, on swiveling brackets, and a tiny vacuum lamp that presently threw a flood of ghastly light upon his terrified face.

He screamed, shrill as a rabbit in a trap, and scuttled out of sight.

Lady Beatrice stepped forward into the circular chamber. Against the far wall was a small bed, a dresser and a washstand. In the midst of the room was a trap door, firmly shut and locked. Beside it was a sort of workbench, on which was what appeared to be a disassembled clock, and it was plain from the tools scattered about that the creature had been working on it when Lady Beatrice entered. The most remarkable thing about the room, however, was its decoration. All around the room's white plaster, reaching as high as ten to twelve feet, were charcoal drawings of machines: gears, pulleys, pistons, springs, wires. Here and there were what seemed to be explanatory notes in shorthand, quite illegible to Lady Beatrice. Nor was she able to discern any purpose or plan to the things depicted.

She walked around the workbench, searching for the room's inhabitant. He was nowhere in sight now, but there beyond the trap door was a chest roughly the size and shape of a blanket-press. Lady Beatrice knelt beside the chest.

"You needn't be afraid, Mr. Rawdon," she said.

From within the chest came a gibbering shriek, which cut off abruptly.

"Leave him alone," said another voice, seemingly out of midair. The illusion was so complete Lady Beatrice looked very hard at the wall, half-expecting to see a speaking tube. "Can't you see you can't talk to Hindley? Go talk to Arthur instead."

"I'm afraid Arthur is dead, Hindley."

"I'm not Hindley! I'm Jumbey. Arthur isn't dead. How ridiculous! Now, you run along and leave poor Hindley alone. He's far too busy to deal with distractions."

"May I speak with you, then, Jumbey? If I promise to leave Hindley alone?"

"You must promise. And keep your promise!"

"I do. I will. Tell me, Jumbey: Hindley builds things, doesn't he?"

"Of course he does! He's a genius."

"Yes, I can see that he must be. He built the levitation device, didn't he?"

"You saw it, did you? Yes. Arthur took it, but Hindley didn't mind. He can always make another."

"Did Arthur ask Hindley to make a levitation device for him?"

"Arthur? No! Arthur's the stupid one. He'd never have come up with such an idea on his own. Hindley was being kept in the little room with the wardrobe. His toys kept rolling under the wardrobe, and poor Hindley couldn't reach them, and nasty Pilkins wouldn't come fetch them for him anymore. So Hindley made something to make the wardrobe float, you see, and then he could always rescue his own toys.

"And then Arthur came home and the servants told on Hindley, and he was so frightened, poor thing, because he was sure it would be the little dark room and the cold water again. But Arthur told Hindley he'd give him a nice big room and a laboratory of his own, if Hindley would make things for him. And Hindley could have all the candy floss he wanted. And Arthur would keep all the strangers away. But he didn't!" The last words were spat out with remarkable venom.

"Didn't he, Jumbey?"

"No! Not a scrap nor a shred of candy floss has Hindley tasted. And there was a big blundering nosey-parker spying on Hindley, down in the tunnels. Hindley had to deal with him all by himself, which was so difficult for poor Hindley, because he can't be seen by people, you know."

"I am so sorry to hear it, Jumbey."

"Arthur is *supposed* to look after Hindley and protect him! Mummy said so. Always."

"Well, Jumbey dear, I'm afraid Arthur can't do that anymore. We will have to make some other arrangement for Hindley."

"Has Arthur gone away to school again?"

Lady Beatrice thought carefully before she spoke. "Yes. He has."

"A-and poor Hindley will be left with Pilkins again?" The confident voice wavered. "Hindley doesn't want that. Hindley doesn't like the little room and the cold water!"

"I believe we can help Hindley, Jumbey."

"How?"

SEVENTEEN:

In which the Ladies Triumph

BLOODY HELL!" EXCLAIMED Mrs. Corvey. Dora, who had just concluded explaining the events of the last two hours, reeled at her language. She glanced around, grateful that Mrs. Duncan had drunk herself into insensibility and the maids had all gone back to their beds, and said: "I'm sure we did our best, ma'am."

"I'm sure you did; but this is a complication, as now there'll be an inquiry. We ain't getting the levitating thing either; I rather suspect it's well on its way to the moon by this time. At least none of that lot upstairs will get it either. Dear, dear, what a puzzle. Where's Lady Beatrice?"

"Here," said she, hurrying down the back stairs quick as a cat. "I am so glad to see you well, ma'am. Did you discover anything?"

"I did, as it happens."

"So did I." Lady Beatrice drew up a kitchen chair and, leaning forward, told her a great deal in an admirably brief time. Mrs. Corvey then returned the favor. Jane, Dora and Maude listened intently, now and then exclaiming in amazement or dismay.

"Well!" said Mrs. Corvey at last. "I think I see a way through our difficulties. Jane, my dear, just go out to the room behind the stable and knock. Ask Mr. Ludbridge if he would be so kind as to step across, and bring the dead Frenchman with him."

PILKINS LOOKED UP with a scowl as Lady Beatrice entered the Great Hall.

"Didn't I tell you hussies to keep to your places below-stairs?" he cried. "The constable will be here any minute!"

"If you please, sir, there's a gentleman arrived in the courtyard, but it's not the constable," said Lady Beatrice. "And I was wondering, sir, if we mightn't just take ourselves off to London tonight, so as to avoid scandal?"

"For all I care you can go to—" said Pilkins, before a solemn knock sounded at the door. He rose to open it. Mr. Ludbridge stood there with a grave expression on his face.

"Good evening; Sir Charles Haversham, Special Investigator for Her Majesty's Office of Frauds and Impostures. I have a warrant for the arrest of Arthur Rawdon, Lord Basmond."

Pilkins gaped. "He—he's dead," he said.

"A likely story! I demand you produce him at once."

"No, he really is dead," said Prince Nakhimov, standing and lifting a corner of the blanket that had been thrown over Lord Basmond's corpse. Ludbridge, who had walked boldly into the Great Hall, peered down at the dead man.

"Dear, dear. How inconvenient. Oh, well; I do hope none of you gentlemen had paid him any considerable sums of money?"

"What d'you mean?" said Sir George Spiggott.

"I mean, sir, that my department has spent the last six months carefully building a case against his late lordship. We have the sworn testimony of no fewer than three conjurors, most notably one Dr. Marvello of the Theater Royal, Drury Lane, that his lordship paid them to teach him common tricks to produce the illusion of levitation. We also intercepted correspondence that led us to believe his lordship intended to use this knowledge to defraud a person or persons unknown."

"But—but—" said Pilkins.

"Good God!" cried Sir George. "A confidence trickster! I knew it! I told him to his face he was a damned un-English bounder—"

"Do you mean to say you quarreled with his lordship, sir?" inquired Lady Beatrice quietly.

"Er," said Sir George. "No! Not exactly. I implied it. I mean to say, I was going to tell him that. In the morning. Because I was, er, suspicious, yes, damned suspicious of his proposal. Yes. I know a liar when I see one!"

"So do I," said Ludbridge, giving him a stern look, at which he wilted somewhat. "And I take it his lordship has died as the result of misadventure?"

"We are waiting for your constabulary to arrive, but *it would appear* Lord Basmond fell down the stairs and broke his neck," said Ali Pasha, with a glance at Sir George.

"Shame," said Ludbridge. "Still, Providence has a way of administering its own justice. None of you were defrauded, I hope?"

"We had as yet not even bid," said Prince Nakhimov.

"Capital! You've had a narrow escape, then. I suspect that my work is done," said Ludbridge. "Much as I would have liked to bring the miscreant into a court of law, he is presently facing a far sterner tribunal."

"If you please, sir," said Pilkins, in a trembling voice. "My lordship wasn't no fraud—"

Ludbridge held up his hand in an imperious gesture. "To be sure; your loyalty to an old family fallen on evil times is commendable, but it won't do, my good man. We have proof that his lordship was heavily in debt. Do you deny it?"

"No, sir." Pilkins's shoulders sagged. The sound of wheels and hoofbeats came from the courtyard. "Oh; that'll be our Ralph bringing the constable, I reckon."

"Very good." Ludbridge surveyed them all. "Gentlemen, in view of the tragic circumstances of this evening, and considering the Rawdons' noble history—to say nothing of your own reputations as shrewd men of the world—I do think nothing is to be gained by bruiting this scandal abroad. Perhaps I ought to quietly withdraw."

"If you only would, sir—" said Pilkins, weeping afresh.

"The kitchens are down here, sir," said Lady Beatrice, leading the way. As they descended, they heard the constable's knock and Ali Pasha saying, "Should someone not go waken the count?"

"A SPLENDID FARRAGO OF lies, sir," said Lady Beatrice, as they descended.

"Thank you. Perhaps we ought to quicken our pace," said Ludbridge. "I should like to be well clear of the house before anyone goes in search of the Frenchman."

"Where did you put him, sir, if I may ask?"

"In his bed, where else? And a nice job someone did on his partner, I must say. Let the Austrians clean that up!"

"Thank you, sir."

"Did anyone hear us?" asked Dora, as they entered the kitchen. "I had to get Jane to help me lift it—not heavy, you know, but awkward."

"They didn't hear a thing," said Lady Beatrice, kneeling beside the chest. "Jumbey? Jumbey, dear, is poor Hindley all right?"

"He's frightened," said the eerie voice. "He can tell there are strangers about."

"Tell him he needn't worry. No one will disturb him, and soon he'll have a bigger and better laboratory to play in."

"Maude, just you go catch your Ralph before he puts the horses away," said Mrs. Corvey, and Maude went running out crying:

"Ralph, my love, would you oblige us ever so much? We just need a ride to the village."

THE TRAGEDY OF Lord Basmond's death set tongues wagging in Little Basmond, but what really scandalized the village was the death of the French count at the hands of his Austrian valet; a crime of passion, apparently, though no one could quite determine how the valet had managed to break all the count's bones. The local magistrate was secretly grateful when an emissary of the Austrian government showed up with a writ of extradition and took the valet away in chains. More: in a handsome gesture, the Austrians paid to have the count's corpse shipped back to France.

Ali Pasha and Prince Nakhimov returned alive to their respective nations, wiser men. Sir George Spiggott returned to his vast estate in Northumberland, where he took to drink and made, in time, a bad end.

When Lord Basmond's solicitors looked through his papers and discovered the extent of his debts, they shook their heads sadly. The staff was paid off and dismissed; every stick of furniture was auctioned in an attempt to satisfy the creditors, and when even this proved inadequate, Basmond Park itself was forfeit. Here complications ensued, with the two most importunate creditors wrangling over whose claim took precedence. In the end the case was tied up in chancery for thirty years.

EIGHTEEN:

In which it is Summed Up

I SAY, LADIES!" HERBERTINA tilted her chair back and rested her feet on the fender. "Here's a bit of news; Basmond Hall has collapsed."

"How awfully sad," said Jane, looking up from the pianoforte.

"Indeed," said Miss Otley. "It was an historic site of great interest."

"It says here it fell in owing to the collapse of several hitherto unsuspected mine shafts beneath the property," said Herbertina.

"I don't doubt it," remarked Mrs. Corvey, with a shudder. "I'm surprised the place didn't fall down with us in it."

"And soon, no doubt, shall be a moldering and moss-grown mound haunted by the spectres of unquiet Rawdons," said Lady Beatrice, snipping a thread of scarlet embroidery floss. "Speaking of whom, has there been any word of poor dear Jumbey?"

"Not officially," said Mrs. Corvey. "There wouldn't be, would there? But Mr. Felmouth has intimated that the present Lord Basmond is developing a number of useful items for Fabrication."

"Happily, I trust?"

"As long as he gets his candy floss regular, yes."

"Jolly good!" Maude played a few experimental notes on her concertina. "Who's for a song? Shall we have 'Begone, Dull Care', ladies?"

THE

BOHEMIAN ASTROBLEME

"OH!" CRIED ENDERLEY'S wife. "The pin has come off my brooch!"

Enderley, lathering his face with soap, grunted and laid down the shaving brush. "Let's see," he said, turning from the washbasin. His wife held out her hand to display the brooch she had inherited from her mother. It was a heavy, old-fashioned thing of silver, set with a large oval stone. The stone looked to be dark red agate, swirled through with fern-like markings. Enderley didn't much care for it, but he was mindful of his wife's stricken expression as he said:

"Easily fixed. We don't need to take it to a jeweler; I can repair it at the laboratory."

"Can you?"

"Of course. Dot of solder will do the job. Set it on the hall table and I'll remember to take it with me."

*E*NDERLEY'S WIFE WAS under the impression he worked for the Patent Office, or some sort of branch of it, doing tests on things. She never asked what, exactly, because she was not of an inquiring disposition. She was content to know that Enderley's weekly wage comfortably furnished their little terrace house in a nicer London suburb and kept all tradesmen's bills current.

When Enderley set forth each morning, beaver hat securely on head and umbrella tightly furled, he did not, in fact, go to the Patent Office nor to any branches it might have. He walked briskly in the general direction of Whitehall, turning in at Craig's Court. He entered an unremarkable mansion of red brick housing one of the less-celebrated clubs in London, Redking's.

Once within its obscure halls, Enderley walked straight past the dining room and bar; passed without a glance the study, where Members dozed in deep chairs or scowled as they perused the *Times*. Enderley walked down a narrow flight of stairs and along a dimly-lit corridor to a pair of doors which, when opened, revealed merely a tiny windowless room within. Enderley stepped inside and closed the doors. Were anyone to open the doors again, assuming at least one minute and fifteen seconds precisely had passed, they would find Enderley nowhere in sight.

This was because Enderley had ridden the Ascending Room down to one of the several storeys that lay concealed beneath Redking's. On one of these subterranean floors, well lit and ventilated by arts currently unknown to the rest of the world, Enderley hung up his beaver hat, set his umbrella in a stand provided for that purpose, donned a white coat, and went to work.

In one respect only were Mrs. Enderley's assumptions correct: Enderley did conduct tests on things. Not, however, on new formulae for aniline dyes or lucifer matches, or improved mechanisms for cotton mills. Rather, Enderley's work on any given day might involve devising new weatherproofing methods for airships, or adapting designs for submarine vessels. In this year of 1845 Jules Verne had as yet written nothing more significant than school compositions, and yet his muse was already alive beneath the pavement of London.

This was because the hidden complex under Redking's housed an ancient fraternity currently known, to those privileged few who knew of its existence, as the Gentlemen's Speculative Society. The Society had gone by other names over the course of its lengthy career. Sir Isaac Newton, Dr. John Dee, and Leonardo da Vinci had all been members. So, it was rumored, had Archimedes and Heron of Alexandria. The Society's goal was the improvement of the human condition through the secret use of *technologia*, until such time as humanity became advanced enough to be made aware of its benefits.

It was generally agreed that some sort of world domination would be necessary before that day arrived, but at the present time the Society was content merely to gather power and pull strings attached to certain government officials. Enderley had been recruited at an early age, after demonstrating his brilliance by winning several prizes. The Society paid him a handsome wage and rewarded especially useful discoveries with generous bonuses, so Enderley was a contented member of the rank and file.

On this particular day Enderley drew the broken brooch from his pocket and set it on his worktable, intending to mend it when he had a moment to spare. As his present project did not involve the use of a soldering iron (he was experimenting with synthetic compounds that showed promise in inducing profound sleep in dogs) the brooch sat forgotten for some hours, until a careless gesture on Enderley's part knocked over a beaker of acetic acid. The acid flooded across several of Enderley's notes and briefly submerged the brooch as well, before finding the edge of the worktable and spattering to the floor.

Muttering to himself, Enderley grabbed a rag and stopped the flood. He pulled his notes free and, whilst waving them in the air, noticed the brooch. He grabbed for it, observing as he did so a peculiar fizzing reaction localized to the ferny inclusions in the red stone. A second later Enderley was lying unconscious and flat on his back where he had been thrown to the floor.

His fellow chemists gathered around him in concern. Judson, who was presently working on a formula to prolong life, stooped to pick up the brooch Enderley had dropped and immediately fell as though poleaxed. Berwick, who was compounding a fuel that might enable steam engines to run without benefit of coal, picked up the brooch and was likewise knocked off his feet, stunned. So was Ponsonby, who had that very morning invented a substance that would enable photographs to be taken and developed in a fraction of the time required by Mssrs. Daguerre or Talbot.

It was left to young Jones, the tea boy, to realize that the best way to pick up the brooch was to gingerly scoop it up between two pieces of pasteboard.

"*I*T'S NOT AN agate," said Greene, pushing the stone across his blotter with the end of a pen. Ludbridge leaned forward and peered at it. Greene customarily prided himself on showing as little emotion as possible during a briefing, and Ludbridge had long since learned that any briefing sessions invariably became contests of sangfroid.

"My dear old chap, gemstones aren't my field of study. I wouldn't know an agate from a bit of red glass."

"As it happens, it *is* a bit of red glass," Greene informed him. "To be precise, it's a tektite."

"And that would be?"

"Meteoric glass. Millennia ago, some monstrous fragment of star-stuff hurtled down and struck the Earth. Sand was melted and re-formed into glassy material, and spewed out across the landscape, to be subsequently buried in other antediluvian upheavals. There's a strewnfield in the Near East with a considerable deposit. There's another in Bavaria. The stuff from the German crater all ended up in Bohemia, and it's called moldavite. This would appear to be a piece of moldavite, but for one thing."

"Mm. What's that?"

"Moldavite's green."

"Well, then it's something else, isn't it?"

Greene shook his head. "Ah, but what? Enderley's asked his wife. The stone was set in a brooch she inherited from her mother. Her mother came from Bohemia. Apparently there's a very rare red variety. Bohemia has its own astrobleme—"

"Beg your pardon?"

"Where's your Latin? Astrobleme, 'star wound'. The impact site of a meteor. The Bohemian one seems to be near Budweis. We think that's the source of the red tektites. We've had Research culling through their references; the red stone is difficult to find, hardly ever comes on the market, and the only written reference we can locate is by a 16th-century alchemist, who gave it the name *blitzstein*."

"Thunder stone? No, no... Lightning stone, wouldn't that be?"

"Yes. Which indicates that someone before Enderley discovered its useful properties." Greene peered down at the stone. "Fortunately for us, no one else seems to have noticed that the red stone, when in contact with acetic acid, generates a powerful electrical charge."

"Useful, I assume?"

"It could be. The chaps in Fabrication are beside themselves at the test results so far. Reliable battery power without jars and jars of stuff in heavy cases. Imagine your field gear powered by a tiny disc of *this*, in a sealed vial of acid. The electric candles, say. Or the thermal goggles."

"Damned useful, then." Ludbridge leaned back, tugging his beard thoughtfully. "Well, what's the job, Greene?"

"We want more of it. All of it, if we can get it." Greene looked directly into Ludbridge's eyes. "You're to go there and see that we do."

"*There* being?"

"Bohemia, where else?" Greene reached out to the globe that sat on the corner of his desk. He spun it briefly and stopped it with a tap of his finger. "Here. You'll be issued maps, of course. You'll have an interpreter and a legman with you."

"Mm. Funds?"

"Parker will make the usual arrangements."

"I mean, are they to be rather more generous than customary? If I'm to buy large quantities of gemstones?"

Greene looked opaque. He stroked his mustache. "Given what's at stake, your allowance is likely to be generous, yes. You are aware, however, that the finance committee lauds every saved halfpenny. Should the opportunity present itself to practice a certain economy, we would, of course, prefer that you take it."

Ludbridge gave a short laugh, aware that such a display of emotion would cost him the match. It was some consolation to see Greene very nearly smirk.

"To be sure! Which one of 'em's a screwsman, the legman or the translator?"

"The legman, naturally. Not our most stable operative, but we've taken steps."

"'Not one of our most stable'…? Who is it?"

"Chap named Hirsch. Talented, but on sufferance just at present."

"I see."

$\mathcal{H}$IRSCH THE LEGMAN was nearly late for the boat train to Dover. Ludbridge and the translator–a small and self-effacing émigré named Ressel–watched as he came running through the crowds at the station. He hurried along the platform, spotted their carriage and pounded on the window, grinning. Ludbridge opened the door. Hirsch swung himself in, threw his solitary bag into the overhead rack and slammed the carriage door as the train began to move.

"So!" He collapsed into his seat and grinned at them once more. "I have arrived."

"Just," said Ludbridge.

"Yes, well, I was having my teeth seen to."

"Were you?" Ludbridge drew out his watch and appeared to consult it.

"Mr. Greene's orders. Lest I should be distracted by the toothache when on the job." Hirsch hooked a finger over his lip and displayed the new silver crown gleaming far back in his mouth.

"Charming," murmured Ressel.

"I am a valuable employee after all, it seems," said Hirsch, with a certain gloating tone.

"Are you?" said Ludbridge. "That matter of the police-man in Whitechapel all a misunderstanding, then?"

Hirsch reddened. He leaned back in his seat and folded his arms. "Naturally you've read some sort of dossier on me, I suppose, since you're the mission leader. Very well! Men make mistakes. And yet, here I am, aren't I? And why is that, do you think?"

"Because you were the best man for the job," said Ludbridge.

Hirsch smiled and laid a finger beside his nose. "Right you are! I track like a hound. And this dog knows a few other tricks, believe me. So all is forgiven and forgotten."

"I expect so," said Ludbridge. "Well, gentlemen. Care for a game of cards?"

*R*AILWAY SERVICE WAS dismal, where it existed at all, in France; rather better in Belgium; varied wildly across the Germanies, necessitating several connections made by horse-drawn coach. They had a long jolting ride from Bavaria to Bohemia before gliding into Budweis via horse-drawn rail car.

"Now for some good beer!" cried Hirsch, as he jumped down and collected his bag. "My father used to cry when he remembered it. Wait until you taste it, Ludbridge! It will open your eyes to that flat warm stuff the English drink. Or perhaps your father was a lord, and didn't drink beer?"

"No; he was a laborer, as it happens. Liked his pint of ale." Ludbridge hoisted out his bag as Ressel jumped down.

They found a hotel for commercial travelers. With rooms secured, they had an excellent meal of pork and dumplings at a biergarten, washed down by beer that Ludbridge admitted, when pressed by Hirsch, was quite good.

"And shall we see the sights first, and set off on our quest tomorrow?" cried Hirsch, whose mood had become more and more ebullient the farther east they had traveled. Insofar as he had borne cheerfully with all the inconvenience of the journey, Ludbridge and Ressel had been grateful, but they had begun to find his high spirits somewhat wearing.

"Don't think it bears discussion at table, do you?" Stolidly Ludbridge helped himself to another slice of dumpling. Ressel glanced nervously over his shoulder.

"In the hotel room, Hirsch," he said in a low voice. "More, er, discreet, yes?"

Hirsch's eyes flashed with anger. He subsided, and consumed the rest of his meal in sullen silence.

LUDBRIDGE AND RESSEL played cards until just before midnight, when Hirsch returned and flung his hat across the room at the hatrack. Missing it, he muttered under his breath as he retrieved it and hung it up.

"And your progress?" Ludbridge folded his hand of cards.

"The red is rare," said Hirsch. "Very rare. Two of the jewelers laughed at me. So did a pawnbroker. This is not employment calculated to increase a man's self-respect."

"Quite," said Ludbridge. "Has anyone got it?"

"One place had a signet ring, another place a woman's pendant with a cameo." Hirsch drew a chair from the group at the table and sat, straddling it front to back. "Priced higher than you wish to pay, perhaps? But you'll see. What I did learn was that both pieces were made by the same man, and the red tektite river flows through him and him alone. Old family business of jewelers, and he is the current inheritor of the firm."

"What's his name?"

"Konrad Bayer." Hirsch felt about in his coat pocket and pulled out a slip of paper, which he handed to Ludbridge. "That is the address of the premises."

"Very good." Ludbridge glanced at it and tucked it away in his waistcoat pocket. "Ressel, you and I will trot round there tomorrow and make a few innocent inquiries."

"Didn't I do a good enough job?" cried Hirsch.

"Of course you did! I'm giving you a day to rest, you damned fool. Chances are you'll have surveillance watch tomorrow night. You'll want all the sleep you can get," said Ludbridge.

THE SHOP BORE a sign reading *BAYER & SOHN*. Behind the display window panes were trays lined in faded velvet, bearing various examples of jewelry design in silverplate and paste. Ludbridge nodded at Ressel and they went in, causing a bell mounted over the door to ring as they did so. Ludbridge, smiling, drew off his hat and bowed to the ancient who rose from behind the counter.

"Tell him I'm pleased to make his acquaintance, and ask him whether he's Herr Bayer."

Ressel translated obediently. The old man shook his head mournfully and replied at length.

"He says he is merely Herr Muller, but he has worked here for forty years and can undoubtedly serve us, as Herr Bayer has not yet come down this morning, and what would the Englishman wish to purchase?"

"Very well; tell him...my wife had a certain brooch, of which she was quite fond, inherited from her Bohemian grandmother, and sadly the stone has gone missing from its setting. It was a particular red glass, not made but naturally occurring, and I have been informed that only here can I purchase a replacement."

Ludbridge watched as Ressel translated again. Even while Ressel was speaking, Herr Muller began to shake his head. He interrupted; Ressel pressed on; they exchanged several brief remarks. At last Ressel turned to Ludbridge.

"He says it is true that Bayer & Son is the only dealer in the red, but they have not had any for a long time now and in fact may not get it in stock again. He suggests you look for it in shops that carry older jewelry, as it sometimes comes up for sale there. Or perhaps you would like to replace it with garnet or ruby."

"Damn. Ask him why they can't get it."

Ressel translated the question. Herr Muller glanced upward once and replied.

"He says he doesn't know, it's none of his business."

"Ask him where the red glass comes from."

The sound of someone descending a staircase came from the rear of the shop. Herr Muller glanced over his shoulder. He said something brief and emphatic.

"He says he doesn't know that either, he is only a clerk, and if you aren't interested in buying rubies or garnets, you had better look elsewhere—"

A man entered the shoproom from a rear door, pulling on a coat as he came. He was tall, reasonably youthful and good-looking, with stylishly curled hair and whiskers, but a certain wolfish and disheveled air. There were circles under his eyes. He looked sharply at Ludbridge and Ressel, and said something in an interrogatory tone to Herr Muller.

Herr Muller replied, sounding stubborn and somewhat affronted. The other addressed himself to Ludbridge and Ressel and spoke forcefully. He turned, said something else to Herr Muller, opened the counter and walked out, letting the counter bang down after him. Taking a hat and walking stick from a stand by the door, he left the shop and walked quickly away. Herr Muller sighed.

"He said some, er, disrespectful things to Herr Muller and he told you that the source of the red is a secret closely held by his firm and when it is to be had he makes announcements in all the papers, and not before. He also told Herr Muller he was going out to get something for his, er, katzenjammer, what you get when you are drinking too much?" Ressel spoke in an undertone.

"Just so." Ludbridge bowed to Herr Muller, replaced his hat and left the shop. Ressel followed like a shadow.

When they were out on the pavement, Ressel said, "I don't think Hirsch is a very nice man."

"Don't you?"

"He's been stealing my socks."

"Mm. Something queer about him, or d'you think he's simply lazy?"

Ressel shrugged unhappily. "He uses my comb too. There was a boy at school like him. Always bullying other boys. Always showing off and defying the schoolmaster."

"Well, don't trouble yourself about it. I'll give you a couple of pounds and you can buy yourself some new socks at a haberdasher's."

"But those were knitted by my mother."

"Steal 'em back then." Ludbridge took out his cigar case and lit a cigar. After a long pause he added: "We can get to Bayer, I think."

"*W*INE, WOMEN AND SONG," said Hirsch, and hiccuped. "Especially women. Herr Bayer spends his money like water! Eats at the best places, so I was obliged to as well–I'll need a little more money, Ludbridge. Has his favorite route that takes him to all the best drinking-places, and I'm not talking about beer. Brandy and champagne for our friend Bayer! And naturally I was obliged to have a drink or two myself, to remain inconspicuous, wasn't I? You see why this is getting a bit expensive.

"And every evening ends the same: the women! But no streetwalkers with muddy skirts for him, no. He goes for the

establishments. When he's had his schnapps
any beauty, respectable ones even, if his eye
1. He's fought four duels in his time. Two mar-
up and a well-born daughter disgraced. It's cost
him a lot of money in lawsuits, I can tell you. An uncontrol-
lable Don Juan!"

"I take it you weren't obliged to spend on similar quality entertainment?" Ludbridge said. Hirsch waved his hand.

"No, but information isn't cheaply bought, either. And
here's a tidbit that cost me two crowns, since you're asking:
his late father was several times approached to engage him in
marriage with assorted daughters of well-to-do merchants.
Having the only knowledge of where the red can be found
makes him desirable, you see? And though he boasts when
he's in his cups, *that* he never brags of. No hints, no oblique
remarks about knowing a big secret, nothing."

"Good to know." Ludbridge tugged at his beard. "An
idiot, in everything but that."

"Precisely." Hirsch grinned wide.

"Very good." Ludbridge rose to his feet. "Well done,
Hirsch."

"Shall I go out again?"

"Not tonight. Get to bed. I'll have work for you tomorrow."

"Ah! Obtaining certain valuables at bargain rates, by
any chance?" Hirsch mimed hitting someone with a cosh.
Ludbridge shook his head.

"Not yet. Fairly soon, I think, but not just yet."

Hirsch bowed mockingly. "I am at your service whenever
required," he said, and left the room.

Ludbridge lit a cigar and waited patiently, listening to the
sounds that indicated Hirsch was retiring: boots pulled off

and dropped, rustle of undress, sounds at the washstand. A dance tune hummed loudly, Ressel's sleepy protest, the tune continuing at a slightly lower volume. Creaking as Hirsch crawled into his bed; snores following fairly soon.

When Ludbridge had finished his cigar, he rose and quietly drew his traveling-bag from under his bed. Opening it, he took out what appeared to be a cigar box, followed by an apparent pair of ear muffs, and at last something that closely resembled one of the brass ear-trumpets used by persons hard of hearing. The brass trumpet fitted into a circular port in the cigar box; Ludbridge unwound a cord from around the ear muffs, slid them on his head, and pushed a sort of aglet on the end of the cord into a second port in the cigar box. Lastly he slid one side of the box upward, after the manner of a Chinese puzzle, revealing beneath a row of small dials and switches.

Turning a switch, Ludbridge saw a tiny red light flash on the panel. He turned one of the dials carefully, hearing as he did so shrill whistles and inorganic screams within what were clearly not earmuffs. After a long moment he spoke into the brass trumpet, in a low and penetrating voice.

"Gentlemen. Gentlemen, Night Operator. Gentlemen. What becomes of illusions?"

A sleepy voice answered in his ear, immediate and yet hollow and echoing with distance. "We dispel them."

"And we are everywhere. Ludbridge communicating. I require a message delivered."

"One moment." Ludbridge fancied he could hear, miles away, the Night Operator scrambling for pen and ink. "Sender, Ludbridge. Recipient?"

"Corvey."

"I *see*. Message?"

"I'll thank you not to take that tone, boy. Message is, 'We require your best. Can pay one-way Urgent Passage for one via Governess Cart. Location is—'" Ludbridge scowled a moment, and then gave the hotel's address.

"Yes, sir. Will that be all, sir?"

"No.... 'Advise, drastic measures possibly called for.'"

"Yes, sir. I'll send that straight over by courier, shall I, sir?"

"Please do."

"Response should be available within two hours, sir."

"Thank you. I shall wait. Ludbridge concluding."

"Gentlemen concluding."

Ludbridge removed the ear apparatus. He got up, walked to the window, stared out at the night awhile; sat down and lit another cigar. When the cigar was out he settled comfortably in his chair, hands clasped across his waistcoat, and fixed his nearly-unblinking gaze upon the transmitting apparatus. Perhaps a quarter of an hour later he saw a green light flash on beside the red one.

Moving with surprising speed for a man of his bulk, Ludbridge crossed the room and pulled on the earpieces.

"Gentlemen? Communicating."

"What becomes of illusions?"

"We dispel them."

"And we are everywhere."

"Ludbridge."

"Response from Corvey, sir."

"And it is?"

"'Expect Lady Beatrice by Governess Cart no later than Wednesday.'"

*I*T WAS CALLED a Governess Cart because it was made to look like one, and in fact it was possible to hitch a pony to its traces and proceed at a modest trot by daylight. Any uninitiated person seeing it might wonder why such a large trunk was crammed under the seat, but few uninitiated persons ever laid eyes on the Governess Cart because it traveled primarily along the deserted highways of the night.

Those few who did glimpse it, generally as they staggered home in an advanced state of inebriation, were never believed if they unwisely spoke of seeing a nocturnal thing with glowing eyes that rocketed down empty lanes at speeds exceeding forty miles an hour, steam engine rattling. The Governess Cart was extremely useful, therefore, as a light priority transport for individuals or packages that simply had to cross distances with greater alacrity than was possible for anyone else in 1845.

Lady Beatrice, who had ridden painfully through the Khyber Pass over the frozen bodies of her father's regiment some years earlier, much preferred speedier means of transportation, and so she quite enjoyed traveling by Governess Cart. It was true that one's hair became wildly disarranged unless one wore a special canvas bonnet tied down and reinforced with hatpins, but Lady Beatrice was well accustomed to wearing specialized clothing. Neither did she mind the goggles nor the long canvas coat recommended for high-speed travelers, since the one kept dust out of one's eyes admirably and the other insulated one against the damps of the night. Lady Beatrice had spent enough time exposed to the damps of the night and was disinclined to suffer them further.

Lady Beatrice was, to put it bluntly, a whore, albeit a well-bred and well-educated one. Being raped by Ghilzai tribesmen had ruined her chances for making a good marriage or, indeed, entering into polite society at all, but fortunately she had encountered the proprietress of a distinguished and exclusive establishment known as Nell Gwynne's. Lady Beatrice now serviced statesmen and diplomats, in the process extracting state secrets and passing them on to Nell Gwynne's fraternal organization, the Gentlemen's Speculative Society. Occasionally blackmail or other, more extreme measures needed to be taken. Lady Beatrice, who had slit the throats of her three Ghilzai assailants and stolen their horses, was equal to specialized work of any kind.

It should be mentioned that she was a tall and slender woman with a chilly autocratic beauty and rather startlingly clear gray eyes. When not traveling abroad, as she was now, she preferred to dress in scarlet. Lady Beatrice was nothing if not honest.

The first faint pallor of dawn had appeared in the east as the Governess Cart crossed from Bavaria into Bohemia. When they were well past the village of Horitz, Mr. Reed, the operator, leaned over sideways to shout over the noise of the engine. "We shan't be able to make much more distance tonight, I'm afraid, but we're nearly there. It will be necessary to get out and walk soon, I'm afraid."

"Shall we walk the rest of the way?"

"Oh, no indeed, madam. As a rule, I simply get between the traces and wait until some farmer passes in a wagon. Generally I spin him a tale about gypsies having stolen my pony, and generally he'll let me tie up to his wagon and ride with him the rest of the way into town."

Conveniently enough, this ruse worked with the first wagon-driving farmer they met, and they rode into Budweis in comfort if not style.

Ludbridge, waiting patiently outside the hotel, saw their approach. He rose, removing his hat. Mr. Reed spoke to the farmer, who paused long enough for Mr. Reed to hand down Lady Beatrice and set her bags on the pavement. Ludbridge took Lady Beatrice's hand and bowed over it, as Mr. Reed and the bemused farmer drove on.

"I trust your journey was uneventful, Ma'am?"

"It was, Mr. Ludbridge. I hope I find you well?"

"You do indeed." Ludbridge picked up her bags. "And very obliging of Mrs. Corvey to spare you on such short notice, I'm sure. Shall we go up to the room for a briefing? I've told the desk clerk my wife was coming for a visit."

Lady Beatrice followed him through the lobby, drawing the startled attention of the clerk, who had imagined Frau Ludbridge would be stout and middle-aged. When Ludbridge paused at the desk to request coffee and breakfast for four sent up, the clerk found himself blushing and stammering like a schoolboy. For some hours afterward he was unable to clear his mind of the gaze of Lady Beatrice's gray eyes.

THAT EVENING THE staff at the Wienhof were similarly affected by the sight of Lady Beatrice, though in their case a certain amount of apprehension was also involved. That a beautiful woman should be dining alone in their establishment was, perhaps, scandalous, but not unusual; a number of the better class of prostitutes were accustomed to plying their trades in the Wienhof, in a low-key and discreet manner.

The staff was at a loss to know quite what to do about this foreign woman, however, who sat at a rear table nibbling biscuits and sipping tea. She did not smile, she did not wink or call out familiarly or in any way employ the signals of her trade. Her appearance, on the other hand, was anything but circumspect. She wore an evening gown of scarlet silk, cut swoopingly low. Her cheeks were rouged scarlet, her lips were scarlet, her gray eyes were rimmed in blackest kohl. She might as well have stood on the table brandishing a placard that advertised her specialties and rates.

Consequently they were much relieved when Herr Bayer arrived for his customary meal and was immediately smitten by the scarlet beauty. He wasted no time in having a glass of champagne sent to her table, and in making eye contact when she had graciously acknowledged him with her thanks. He followed up with an invitation to dine at his table, which she accepted. He ordered the finest (and most expensive) meal the Wienhof provided, partridges in a sauce of brandy and cream, and during the meal trotted out his entire repertory of seductive phrases. The woman appeared receptive, smiling demurely and replying in schoolroom German. Herr Bayer seemed to find this quite charming.

So intent were the staff in watching the little comedy play itself out, and so intent was Herr Bayer on the thrill of the chase, that none of them wasted a thought on the pair of gentlemen seated across the room. One was an Englishman with somewhat blunt and leonine features, who seemed interested in nothing but his plate of Wiener schnitzel, rotkohl and spaetzle. The other was a timid-looking fellow who picked at his dish of rouladen. Neither of them looked up when Herr Bayer shouted for a waiter, nor when he demanded whether a room was available upstairs. Nor were they distracted from their meal when Herr Bayer and his inamorata rose from the table and retired to an upper floor of the Wienhof.

It was noticed, however, that the two gentlemen dawdled lengthily after finishing their entrees. They requested coffee. They requested two helpings each of hazelnut torte. They requested after-dinner liqueurs, and seemed content to sit for hours, nursing their glasses of kirsch and chatting quietly.

HERR BAYER, HAVING ridden to bliss three times in succession, sagged sideways and collapsed into the feather bed. Lady Beatrice smiled and shifted sideways to face him.

"Such splendid endurance!" she murmured.

"God in heaven, I'm like a greedy child in a sweets shop," said Herr Bayer. He pulled her close and crushed her against him, kissing her ravenously. Lady Beatrice endured his attentions with perfect ease, showing neither revulsion nor discomfort. She had long since grown accustomed to detaching herself from the things her body was obliged to do, and during Herr Bayer's recent frenzied passion had been fondly recalling a recent holiday in the Lake District.

Now, however, she became aware that the present tussle had revived Herr Bayer's tumescence. He released her and looked down at himself.

"Bah! The naughty thing wants attention again. And what am I to do, my beauty? I faint with exhaustion. I will have to wear a hot poultice on my back tomorrow, I'm certain

I've sprained something. But perhaps you would like to eat some sausage? Eh?" Herr Bayer leered as he ground his hips against hers suggestively.

"I have a better idea," said Lady Beatrice, smiling as she pushed him back. "But first, shall we have another glass of champagne?"

"Play Hebe, my fair one, and pour the flowing wine!"

Lady Beatrice turned and sat up on the edge of the bed. A single languorous gesture, like a cat stretching, enabled her to reach the tumbled mass of her clothes and pluck what appeared to be a small glass button from the waistband of her crinoline. Palming it, she rose and dropped the button in one of the pair of champagne glasses on the bedside table. She refilled the glasses, waiting only to assure herself that the button had dissolved without a trace before handing the glass to Herr Bayer.

"Prost, Herr Stallion."

"Prost, my Queen of Sheba!"

They clinked glasses and drank. Lady Beatrice set her glass aside after a sip and, with slow deliberation, moved to straddle Herr Bayer.

"Now, my dear, you lie there at your ease and rest your back. I will deal with the naughty creature."

Rising above him, she did something–again, slowly and consideringly–that made Herr Bayer's toes curl. He gasped, whooped, gulped down the rest of his champagne and hurled the empty glass across the room, where it shattered against the wall and dropped to the floor in a shower of sticky crystal fragments.

"Yes!" he screamed. "Yes, my adored, my little cat, my sugar cake!"

Lady Beatrice continued to do what she had been doing, settling into a steady rhythm. Herr Bayer writhed underneath her, fumbling and squeezing at her breasts. She gazed steadily into his eyes and saw the gradual look of happy idiocy that came into them. His hands fell away from her breasts; rose again to bat at them as a feeble kitten bats at catnip mice, before finally falling back to lie on either side of his head. He had begun to drool slightly.

Lady Beatrice wiped the drool away with a corner of the sheet. Herr Bayer giggled.

"I understand you are a jeweler, my dear Herr Bayer."

"That's so." He emphasized his reply with a nod.

"You used to sell that particular red gemstone, the meteor-glass, the sort that only Bayer and Son can procure."

"Of course! We will again. All it'll take is a crop failure… season without rain…hoof and mouth disease, you will see, sooner or later the Reithoffers will need money and then they'll come with a big box of it, hat in hand. You'll see. This is always the way it is."

"And who are the Reithoffers, my dear?"

"Farmers. Nobodies. But they own the secret mine, you see?"

"They obtain the red glass from a mine on their property?"

"Yes."

"And their mine is the only source?"

"Of course. We have tried for a hundred and seventy years to find any other. We might as well have been look-ing for fairy…pancakes." Herr Bayer giggled again. "Not, nothing, none, never, nowhere. Only the damned Reithoffers know where it is. It's quite unfair."

"Why do they only mine the stone when they need money?"

"Because they are superstitious peasants," Herr Bayer replied. "'*Ach, mein herr, the mine is cursed! Every third man who goes in to dig for the stone, the Witch gets him! The Witch got great-great-uncle Hans, and Grandfather Horst, and Uncle Wilhelm!* Boo hoo hoo!'"

"And they will not sell the land?"

"No. It is their land. They are farmers, what else would they do? They are too stupid to learn even, even...shoemaking. You have no idea of their stubbornness. The pigs." Herr Bayer tried to spit, and the blob so produced ended up in his own eye. He laughed uproariously at that. Lady Beatrice wiped his eye with more of the sheet.

"And where exactly is their land, my very dear Herr Bayer?"

"Behind Sinietsch," he replied promptly. "Beyond the woods. They keep to themselves. Only the kobolds keep them company. Live like bears. Anyone in the village will agree with me. It's because of the terrible, shameful curse..."

His voice gurgled away into silence. His stare was becoming steadily glassier.

"You have been an exceedingly good boy, Herr Bayer," said Lady Beatrice. "You have earned a reward."

She accelerated her movements, which sent Herr Bayer into a flailing ecstasy so extreme it quite extinguished the last spark of his consciousness. As he was sinking gratefully into a black velvet-lined void, Lady Beatrice climbed briskly from the bed and washed her face clean of its smeared paint at the washbasin. She put on her undergarments and spent a moment patiently turning her gown inside out, the gown being made in such a way that it was reversible: scarlet silk with watered gray silk lining or watered gray silk with scarlet silk lining. After dressing herself, she exited the room quietly, closed the door behind her, and descended the stairs, a shadowy and respectable ghost of her former self.

Herr Bayer slept like the dead until the chamber-attendant brought hot water next morning. He sat bolt upright in bed, looking around for Lady Beatrice; was briefly relieved not to find her, since he preferred whores to decamp before sunrise; was next panicked, and sought frantically through his clothing until he located his purse; next was astonished to discover, as he hurriedly counted his money, that this particular whore had apparently neglected to collect her fee on departing; next was elated, on re-counting his funds, to confirm this suspicion. Herr Bayer whistled as he dressed himself and went downstairs to order breakfast.

He had no memory whatsoever of anything he had told Lady Beatrice, after that last glass of champagne.

$\mathcal{L}$UDBRIDGE UNROLLED A map and regarded it. "To be sure. Sinietsch. I expect the Reithoffers' farm must be somewhere *here...*"

"I believe the phrase used was 'beyond the woods'," said Lady Beatrice. She was the only person other than Ludbridge himself who was actually looking at the map. Ressel kept his gaze fixed on his shoes, and Hirsch stared hungrily at Lady Beatrice.

"Indeed. Right, Hirsch–this is your meat. You're to go to Sinietsch today and find out what you can. Pay a call on the Reithoffers, under some pretext. Report back this evening."

"On one condition," said Hirsch coyly. Ludbridge looked up at him, affronted.

"What the deuce do you mean?"

"I want a kiss to send me on my way."

"Come here and I'll give you a good one," replied Ludbridge, with only a hint of thunder in his tone. Hirsch turned red.

"I meant from our beauty here. Surely she won't mind a little merchandise given away free?"

Ludbridge stared at him, flint-eyed. Lady Beatrice cleared her throat.

"Mr. Hirsch, I think you misunderstand. I am not a commodity. I am a specialist, just as you are. My particular skills serve the same ends, but by different means."

"Then you should kiss me," said Hirsch. "Since that's my price for the day's work."

Ressel groaned and put his head in his hands. Ludbridge rose slowly to his feet, but Lady Beatrice put up her hand.

"It's a trivial enough request. Very well, Mr. Hirsch." She rose to her feet. He jumped up at once and came to her, licking his lips. She kissed him. He grabbed her in his arms and attempted to wrestle with her, groping her bosom, laughing muffledly, but abruptly broke off and backed away from her. Lady Beatrice, who had produced a small pistol apparently from thin air and pressed it under his ear, returned to her seat.

"I don't believe you should attempt to do that again, Mr. Hirsch," she said composedly. "Please understand that the only pleasure I derive from my duty is the satisfaction of knowing what it will accomplish. We are all working toward the same great day, are we not?"

"Bitch," said Hirsch. He strode to the door, grabbed his coat, and turned back briefly to address Ludbridge. "You may not like me, but you will see what work *I* can do."

He slammed the door behind him, and they heard him charging down the stairs.

"How juvenile," said Lady Beatrice, at the same moment Ressel cried, "Fraulein, a thousand apologies–you mustn't think we're all beasts–" and Ludbridge gave a wordless growl.

"That is quite all right, Mr. Ressel," said Lady Beatrice, smiling at him. "It's of little consequence. I have dealt with far worse than Mr. Hirsch."

"Well, what are you waiting for?" Ludbridge demanded of Ressel. "Go in there and steal your socks back."

$\mathscr{R}$ESSEL HAD PLENTY of time to retrieve his socks and his comb too, for that matter, because Hirsch failed to return that evening. Ludbridge stalked the floor for hours before giving up and sleeping on the divan, having relinquished his bed to Lady Beatrice. Hirsch still had not put in an appearance by the time Ludbridge went down to order breakfast for three. As he was about to return to the rooms, the clerk turned to the back counter with a little cry.

"I nearly forgot! Herr Ludbridge, a letter has come for you. A courier delivered it this morning." He drew it from its pigeonhole and held it out. Ludbridge took it.

"Thank you." Ludbridge studied it as he climbed the stairs. He did not recognize the hand in which it was addressed, but as he opened it and read its contents he certainly recognized the tone.

My old Ludbridge,

I write to you from Sinietsch, which has, as
it turns out, a splendid tavern and marvelously
accommodating women. But you must not think
I put pleasure before business. Here is what I have
accomplished for you:

Having arrived here, I was able to locate direc-
tions to the Reithoffer farm immediately. As I was
passing the tavern I chanced upon a peddler with a
tray of the sorts of things such people sell, and luckily
for me he set the tray down in an inattentive moment
while washing his face at a fountain. So prepared, I
set off for the farm.

You never saw such a countrified place in your
life–a little cart-track off a mountain road, winding
through the trees to a gate, and huge savage barking hounds who wanted to tear me limb from limb.
I prudently remained on my side of the gate and
before long a surly peasant came down to see why
his hounds were making such a fuss. I tipped my hat
and displayed my riches, at which he tied up the dogs
and bid me enter.

I followed him through the cabbage fields to the
house, and such a scene from the dark ages when we
got inside! Absolutely old Bohemia, with a couple
of ancients by the fire and a brat or two staggering
about and a bevy of peasant women busy putting
up sauerkraut in stone crocks. The shelves were
positively lined with crocks of pickles and more
sauerkraut. You may imagine that the maidens were
frantic for something other than pickles with which

to divert themselves, and so I and my wares were eagerly received.

Of course, I sold at bargain prices! Spools of thread, bits of lace, ribbons, pins, a pair of scissors, a songbook of tunes that were out of fashion thirty years since and a cheap chromolithograph of Our Lord Jesus Christ, all found favor in the sauerkraut girls' eyes. So much so that I was invited to dine. The men of the house were less pleased to see me. Imagine hulking cousin-marrying peasants in boots fresh-caked with mud of the fields and less pleasant substances, all lined up at a long trestle, eyeing me suspiciously.

The fare was minuscule pork cutlets, massive flour dumplings, even bigger helpings of the eternal sauerkraut, and not even a good beer to wash any of this down, but thin sour cider! Pity poor me, Ludbridge, where you sit at your ease in civilized Budweis. Anyway I could see there was no use trying to get any secrets out of these mountain trolls, so I waited until after they had gone to the fields and managed to get one of the younger girls alone for a little romance. She was eager enough until I asked her about a story I'd heard concerning witches in the forest. That closed up her lips so tight I could see there was no use pursuing it (or her) further, so I tipped my hat and took my leave.

But the good people of Sinietsch were willing to talk, I can tell you, when I got back into town (without my peddler's tray, of course; that I disposed of in a convenient ditch). With a liberal largesse to the tavern patrons, this I learned:

The Reithoffer land is indeed cursed, or so I was solemnly assured. There is a Witch who haunts the place and every generation or so she takes one of the Reithoffer men for a lover, though this act has immediate consequences for the unfortunate male as he is always found dead and singed with hellfire following her embrace. Why the Witch is up there no one knows for certain, but the clearest story I heard was that there is cursed buried treasure somewhere on the Reithoffer farm, and there the Witch haunts. Some are of the opinion that her lovers came seeking the treasure and paid the price. The last time this happened was within living memory, in 1839.

I did not go back to search for the mine because, what was I to do about the dogs? And, really, I have worked hard enough for one day. I am going to take a little holiday now for a few days, until the expense money runs out. I close now because the post rider waits, but perhaps I will tell you where I am later.

Cheerfully,
Hirsch.

Crumpling the letter in his fists, Ludbridge swore quietly.

SINIETSCH WAS EASILY reached in a rented gig. Ressel drove. Ludbridge sat beside him, mulling over what he felt he could trust of Hirsch's report. Lady Beatrice, dressed in respectable gray once more, sat quietly in the back and enjoyed viewing the passing countryside. At last Ludbridge turned to her.

"Do you reckon you could portray an hysteric?"

"How hysterical do you require me to be, Mr. Ludbridge?"

Ludbridge thought about it. "Not excessively. Not weeping-and-wringing-your-hands hysterical."

"More of a fainting-fit-for-unspecified-female-disorders hysterical? I believe I can manage that, yes, Mr. Ludbridge."

When they drove at last up the main street of Sinietsch, Ludbridge looked for village taverns. There was only one, as it happened, and he bid Ressel pull up before it.

"Go in and ask whether Hirsch is staying here. You might find out if there's a doctor about, as well."

Ressel went in, and returned a few minutes later, looking rather harried.

"Hirsch is no longer there. He left suddenly and owing money. The proprietors were very angry, so I told them I was a debt collector trying to trace him. They were much more helpful after that. Dr. Schildkraut's house is at the end of that lane." Ressel pointed.

Ludbridge chewed his cigar. "What the devil does Hirsch think he's playing at? Still in school and scoring off the headmaster? Well, on to the Doctor's."

They pulled up in front of a modest half-timbered house. "Any objection to feigning illness for a good twenty minutes or so?" Ludbridge asked Lady Beatrice.

"None whatsoever, Mr. Ludbridge." Lady Beatrice put the back of her hand to her head and sprawled back on her seat, fluttering her eyelids.

"I'm obliged to you, Ma'am."

Dr. Schildkraut was an elderly man who opened his own door. He gaped rather at the sight on his doorstep: an Englishman supporting a swooning Englishwoman, and a smaller man, very agitated, asking whether the doctor was available to examine the fraulein, who had suffered an attack of the vapors. He ushered them into his parlor, and after a series of hastily translated questions determined that he ought to see the fraulein in his examining room. Thither she was led, drooping on the arm of the Englishman–Dr. Schildkraut assumed he was her father–who, upon seeing her safely disposed in a chair, tipped his hat and departed to wait in the parlor.

Once the door had closed, Ludbridge strode to a bookcase on the wall, wherein sat a number of bound leather volumes. Years were painted on their spines, in a small precise hand.

"Here's the one," said Ludbridge, pulling out the journal for the year 1839. Ressel came and peered over his shoulder as he leafed through it. "We're looking for the name Reithoffer."

They flipped the pages, passing births, illnesses, recoveries and death in Sinietsch. Near the end of the book Ressel grabbed Ludbridge's arm and pointed. "Here!"

"What's it say?" Ludbridge peered at the page.

"Says, er... 'Last night Frau Kohl came to me in fear. She was attending one of the Reithoffer girls who has gone into early labor and the baby will not turn. We went together to the Reithoffer farm and arrived at daybreak. Just as we were driving up we saw that one of the men was out by the house digging what looked like a grave. I asked if the girl had already died but Frau Kohl told me the grave was for another member of the family who had been found dead the day before, which she thought had sent the young mother into her pangs.'

"Then he says...er...a lot about bringing the baby into the world. They saved the mother and child. And then, he goes into the kitchen and he sees...well, there is a body the old people are washing for burial. He asks to examine it because he has heard of this curse, you see. Dead man is the girl's uncle, 'Peter Reithoffer, forty years of age, well-nourished, appearance of a corpse struck by lightning. Fernlike burn patterns on the skin.' Doctor asks if he was struck by lightning, family is looking, er, shamefaced. They say he is marked with the Witch's mark and was taken in accordance with his sin. Doctor asks, what sin? Family elder replies, he died in the embrace of the Witch. So that is why he can't be buried in consecrated ground. They won't tell him more. He leaves...he gives Frau Kohl a ride back to her house and she tells him, when they brought in the dead man his trousers were down around his thighs, like all the others killed by the curse."

"Bloody hell," murmured Ludbridge. "Fern patterns. Anything more?"

"He just says he is sorry people can believe in such nonsense in this age and he thinks it was lightning all the same."

"Didn't ask what the man was doing when he died?"

"No, apparently." Ressel, a little red-faced, closed the book and put it back in its place. They sat down on a bench clearly provided for anxious relatives. Ressel twiddled his thumbs while Ludbridge smoked and thought.

"Fernlike patterns," he muttered at last. "Yes, I've seen that. Seaman on the *Tiger* struck by lightning whilst aloft.

Extraordinary coincidence…" He was silent another moment and then slapped his knee.

"I'll tell you what it is, Ressel. Why's a man take his prick out of his trousers, eh? What's the most common reason?"

Ressel blushed once more. "To, er, make water, I suppose."

"Precisely. And let's say a man feels the call of nature when he's down in a mine. Is he going to walk all the way out and water the nearest tree, or is he just going to make water right there in the mine?"

"I… suppose he would make water in the mine."

"So." Ludbridge took his cigar out of his mouth. "Just exactly how much acetic acid's in the urine of a man who lives on sauerkraut, pickles and cider?"

Ressel considered that a moment. His eyes widened in horror.

"*That's* how the damned fools have been killing themselves," said Ludbridge, chuckling. He broke his laughter off abruptly when the examining room door opened and Lady Beatrice emerged, leaning on the doctor's arm. Ludbridge escorted Lady Beatrice out to the gig, while Ressel paid the doctor.

"A mild case of hysteria," Dr. Schildkraut told him in a low voice. "Give her fresh air and a few novels and she will be perfectly well. You know what these women are."

*I*T WAS A simple enough matter, thereafter, to field-test Enderley's Improved Canine Stupefaction Compound on the Reithoffers' immense snarling hounds. The Compound proved to work a treat, enabling Ludbridge and Ressel to don night-vision goggles and explore the Reithoffers' considerable acreage without fear of detection. The mine was easily located at the distant edge of the farm, though the track leading to it was overgrown and its entrance masked with tall weeds. Once entered and inspected, it proved to bear rich veins of the red tektite.

Somewhat more complicated was stage-managing the business of the thunder-machine and lightning flashes. Lady Beatrice's appearance as the Witch necessitated recourse to her scarlet gown and moreover to her cosmetics case, in order to provide the fernlike facial markings. It was particularly felicitous that she happened to own, among a number of colored glass lenses designed to give her eyes a striking appearance, a scarlet pair; for, as she pointed out, one never knew what sort of peculiar fantasies (being seduced by a vampyre, for example) members of Parliament might request.

The Reithoffers, suitably frightened by the spectacle of their family's ancient persecutor appearing in the front garden, readily obeyed her demand that they venture into town and sell that corner of their property containing the tektite mine to a certain Englishman they would find in the tavern. Ludbridge gave them a good price. They congratulated themselves on making a tidy profit on the deal and incidentally unloading their family curse on somebody else.

"*T*HAT MINE WAS one of the most disturbing places I have ever had the occasion to have seen," said Ressel, as they climbed down from the gig. "Didn't you think? Like, er, the throat of a whale, with all that redness."

"Well, you won't be obliged to go back in, I shouldn't think," said Ludbridge, handing Lady Beatrice and her cosmetics case down. "All that's left for *us* to do is get the title deed back to London and file a report."

"I do hope Mr. Hirsch has come to his senses and is waiting for us at the hotel," said Lady Beatrice, as they crossed the street. Ludbridge scowled.

"I'll have a few things to say about *him*, by God. He'd better be there."

"Er...there are rather a lot of police about this morning," said Ressel, looking around uneasily.

As they stepped within, the desk clerk saw Ludbridge and waved.

"Herr Ludbridge? A parcel and a letter for you."

Collecting them, Ludbridge noted Hirsch's handwriting. He sighed and shook the small box experimentally; only a faint rattle gave any idea of its contents. In a casual tone he remarked: "Rather a lot of police in the street, aren't there?"

"There have been two robberies!" said the clerk. "Both in one night! Herr Kimmel the jeweler and Herr Lantz the pawnbroker, both robbed of hundreds of marks in goods. Herr Lantz is in bed with a fractured skull."

"What a dreadful thing," said Ludbridge. He went upstairs, followed by Lady Beatrice and Ressel.

Ressel went into his room to pack his bag; Lady Beatrice seated herself in a chair by the window, gazing out, as Ludbridge opened the box. He shook its contents into his hand and swore. Lady Beatrice looked at him inquiringly. He held out a signet ring and a cameo pendant, both set with red tektite stones.

"That's all we had found here in Budweis," said Ludbridge. "But I hadn't given him the word to do the burglary yet."

"Hirsch's bag is gone," said Ressel, appearing in the doorway.

"Oh, dear," said Lady Beatrice. Ludbridge ground his teeth and opened the letter.

> *My very dear Ludbridge,*
>
> *This letter serves as notice that I have, after much reflection, decided to take my talents to more appreciative (and better-paying) masters than the Gentlemen. However, do not despair! Here as a token of good faith are the bits of red tektite I found for you. I got them at a bargain price...however, you may wish to find a way to conceal them from the customs agents. You may find things a trifle hot in Budweis now, also, until the police find someone to arrest for my little indiscretion, but do not fear; I am sure the Gentlemen can easily arrange for your release, if worst comes to worst. I myself intend a swift departure.*
>
> *Please convey to the Gentlemen that I will soon communicate a postal location where my wages may be sent, as well as the monthly stipend I expect for my silence on the matter of the red tektite's astonishing properties. A hundred pounds a month is not too much, I think, considering the value of the information and the delight with which it would be received by certain interested governments.*

> *Farewell, old man, and a big wet ravishing kiss*
> *with my tongue for the lady in red. Or perhaps some-*
> *thing more. I leave it to her imagination.*
> *Your much undervalued friend,*
> *Hirsch*

"That's done it." Ludbridge folded the letter and tucked it inside his coat. He drew out his watch, thumbed a button on its side, and studied it a moment. "That stupid son of a bitch. Your pardon, ma'am, but he's run off, or so it would appear. Ressel, finish packing. Ma'am, can you be ready to depart within the next ten minutes?"

"Certainly." Lady Beatrice rose to her feet.

"Good." Ludbridge bounded upright and began packing with breathtaking speed.

$\mathcal{T}$HEY DEPARTED THE hotel a few bare minutes before the police descended on it to question all foreign visitors, or so Ludbridge learned later. At the time he was not disposed to be communicative about his reasons for flight; as they hurried toward the horse-rail station he kept checking his watch. Only when they were seated in the car was Ressel able to lean forward and look at the watch face.

"But that is not a clock," he remarked in surprise. "That is a little map of Budweis!"

"So it is," said Ludbridge, chuckling. "D'you see the tiny red light flashing there? That's our friend Hirsch. One doesn't cross the Gentlemen, you see."

"I just saw him," said Lady Beatrice in a low voice. "He's here. He hid behind the kiosk when he saw us. I can still see his boots and the corner of his bag."

"I should look away if I were you, ma'am," said Ludbridge.

He gave his watch stem a quarter-turn and depressed it. There was a *bang* followed by screams and shouting. Glancing over at the kiosk, he saw the fan-splatter of blood. Bits of Hirsch's head began to fall hither and yon. The silver molar crown, that had concealed the tracking mechanism and explosive, landed with a particularly musical tinkle on the cobbles not four feet away.

"That'll teach him," said Ludbridge, and lit a cigar. Ressel stared at him in horror. Lady Beatrice shrugged regretfully and took out her knitting.